# Junctions

# *Junctions*

## Daniel Mandishona

First published by
Weaver Press, Box A1922, Avondale, Harare, 2018
<www.weaverpresszimbabwe.com>

Typeset by Weaver Press
Cover Design: Daniel Mandishona, Jr.
Photo (p.v) © Weaver Press
Printed by Running Rat, Harare
Distributed in South Africa by Jacana Media, Johannesburg

ISBN: 978-1-77922-343-2 (p/b)
ISBN: 978-1-77922-344-9 (e-pub)

**DANIEL MANDISHONA** is an architect. He was born in Harare in 1959 and brought up by his maternal grandparents in Mbare township (then known as Harari township). In 1976 he was expelled from Goromonzi Secondary School and lived in London from 1977-1992. He first studied Graphic Design then Architecture at the Bartlett School, University College London. He now has his own practice in Harare. His first short story, 'A Wasted Land' was published in *Contemporary African Short Stories* (Heinemann,1992). He has since been published by Weaver Press in *Writing Now* (2005), *Laughing Now* (2007) *Writing Free* (2011) and *Writing Lives* (2014). He also published a collection of short stories, *White Gods. Black Demons* (Weaver Press, 2009).

# Contents

# Butterflies in the Rain

*Childhood is the kingdom where nobody dies.*
Edna St. Vincent Millay

*21st March, 2008*

It was a week before the end of the first term. Schools were to be closed early to allow teachers to be employed as polling agents in the forthcoming election. The heavy downpour had stopped as abruptly as it had begun. A rainbow straddled the distant horizon, its colours diffused by the soft glow of sunset. Anxious not to soil their shoes and khaki uniforms, Robert and Nhamo Muswe hopped, skipped and jumped over the puddles of brown water along the narrow path. Robert, at thirteen, was two years older than his brother. Their best friends, the Makupa boys – Sylvester, Noah and Martin – had not been to school since the previous week, which was unusual. There had been an outbreak of mumps at their school, and Robert and Nhamo wondered if the Makupa boys had become the latest victims.

Robert suggested to Nhamo that they take a detour and go and check on the boys at their home, about two kilometres from their own. Nhamo was uncomfortable with the idea, remembering how their widowed mother had told them to come straight home after school each day.

'We'll tell her we were catching butterflies in the rain for the Nature Study lessons,' said Robert.

Reluctantly, Nhamo nodded his head. He knew it was not a good idea to disobey their strict mother, but he had faith in his elder brother as they often did their mischief together. Robert was jealously protective of his brother, a slow learner who suffered from albinism, and always stood up for him in times of crisis.

The election was several days away but there had been several cases of politically motivated violence in the neighbouring villages, which was the reason why their mother worried about them staying out late. Although tender in years, the boys had already experienced the trauma caused by political strife. A year previously their own father, Orgreave Muswe, had been killed during an altercation at the local business centre. There had been numerous witnesses to the incident, but nobody had ever been charged with the crime. At a rally for the ruling party held at their school the previous month, Sly's father, Lazarus Makupa, had been denounced by the village headman for being a 'sell-out' and for secretly supporting the opposition party. The violence had jarred the tranquillity of the Muswe boys' rural lives.

Aware there was still about an hour of daylight, the two boys started walking in Indian file in the direction of the Makupa homestead. Nhamo, who liked showing off, started reciting a poem his Grade Five class had learnt that day during the English lesson.

'*Twas brillig, and the slithy toves did gyre and gimble in the wabe...*'

Robert tried to catch some butterflies, to justify their expected late arrival home. But the colourful creatures were too quick and Nhamo kept laughing at his brother's spirited but clumsy efforts. When they arrived at the homestead, the first thing the boys noticed was that all the homestead's four huts had been razed by fire. The flimsy farm-brick walls had been blackened and cracked by the heat. Standing at a distance, Robert shouted out his friend's name, but there was no response. With their hearts pounding, they cautiously approached the seemingly deserted homestead. The half a dozen cattle Mr Makupa owned were locked up in the kraal. The agitated beasts watched the intruders with mild bemusement. The Makupa family's twenty-odd black and white goats milled silently outside their pen, as if waiting for somebody to herd them in. The first hut the boys went to was the one where Sly and his two younger brothers slept. Flies were buzzing everywhere and there were fat maggots on the floor. Nhamo, sweating with fear, gently tugged his brother's elbow.

'Come, Robbie... Let's go home. Mother will be getting worried by now...'

'Soon. Let's just look into the other huts.'

'Robbie..?'

'Nothing will happen to us.'

The hut used as the family kitchen was in a similar state to the boys' bedroom. Cooking utensils discoloured by soot were strewn all over the floor. The thatched roof, like those on other huts, had been reduced to a mound of ash on the floor and all that remained of an old double sofa was its skeletal frame. A few charred roof trusses dangled precariously above the boys' heads. A pair of crows that had taken to a nearby tree stared disinterestedly at the new arrivals. But the silence was unnerving.

'Robbie, please. Let's leave now. Sly's not here, Noah's not here, Martin's not here. There's nobody here. Mother will be angry with us...'

A watery-eyed mongrel stared at them from the threshold of what remained of the homestead's main hut, before hesitantly shying away on their approach. Even the granary had been razed to the ground, with the wooden stilts upon which it had been raised now calcified stumps. The boys, speechless and scared, stared at the sad devastation. At the back of the granary they found a solitary vulture pecking at an object on the ground. Although daylight was fast fading, both boys could clearly see what the bird was pecking at. Recognising the lower mandible of a human skull from their Nature Study lessons, the boys ran off screaming into the gathering gloom.

By nightfall, the story of the arson attack at the Makupa

homestead had spread far and wide. Nobody, it seemed, knew what had happened to the family, but people had their suspicions. The following morning, a policeman came to the Muswe homestead. He was accompanied by the village headman, who had been informed of the boys' grisly discovery by their irate mother the previous evening. Robert told the policeman that five people lived at the Makupa homestead – Mr Lazarus Makupa and his wife Angeline, their twelve-year old son Sylvester and his two younger brothers – Noah and Martin.

On their way back from school at lunchtime the two boys, driven by curiosity, once again disobeyed their mother and went to the Makupa homestead. 'We'll tell mother that we had to catch locusts for the Nature Study lesson,' Robert assured his younger sibling. Three policemen, wearing face masks and white gloves, were casually picking up the human bones that had been scattered by wild animals all over the homestead, and placing them into a metal coffin in the back of an unmarked truck. The cattle, still locked up in their kraal, watched the policemen with little interest. Nhamo nervously tugged at Robert's hand, indicating they should leave. As they walked, he started mumbling the poem the Grade Five class had learnt during the English lesson the previous day, his voice now trembling with his sadness.

'*All mimsy were the borogoves, and the mome raths outgrabe...*'

# 1

## Of Heroes and Paupers

Paul had often seen the toothless old lady at the same intersection. Every morning, she would suddenly appear by the driver's window and ask him for help. And in the evenings, when he drove back to his flat on the periphery of the city centre, she would be there again, begging for money or food. At first, he felt sorry for her and would part with a few coins. They had little value, and he had no qualms parting with them. Sometimes he would even give her the leftovers from his numerous business lunches. He never hesitated to ask for a doggy bag even when someone else was paying.

But over the years, he noticed that he was the only one giving her money. Other motorists would ignore the old lady and make sure their windows were closed whenever she approached their vehicles. They seemed to regard her as an avoidable irritant. That was when Paul had hardened himself and stopped giving her money and, like the other motorists, he would shout at her to stop bothering people and do something worthwhile. She would just give him a benign smile and shake her head. Sometimes she would say 'God bless you, my son', before moving on to the next vehicle. But Paul's remonstrations didn't stop her from coming to the driver's window every time his car pulled up at the intersection. Then his mother, who had endured a heart condition for many years, suddenly passed away.

The funeral was at the house of Paul's older brother, Lawrence. It was attended by most of their relatives and his mother's religious friends. Even Paul's sister, Hannah, who had been in the diaspora for many years, took time off work and managed to arrive in time for the burial. The day they laid their mother to rest, intermittent rain interrupted the smooth flow of the programme. And it was then that Paul briefly spotted the old beggar talking to several female mourners in the main tent. He noticed that she wore an old *doek* in the colours of the ruling party, as did the women to whom she was talking. Indeed, she was the most talkative of the group, and her audience seemed to be listening attentively. Paul made a mental note to look for her later and ask her how she had known his late mother. He was intrigued, and pleasantly surprised. His mother had been a staunch church-goer and knew many people in the community. The day after the burial, Paul's closest relatives, as per their clan's customs, sat in the lounge and shared out his late mother's earthly possessions. Paul was given one of his mother's old winter jumpers. He smiled a little wryly knowing that he had bought her the jumper with his first pay from his first job many years before. Later that day, Paul and Lawrence drove their sister Hannah to the airport for her return journey to San Francisco.

The following day, Paul's life resumed its well-trodden routine to his offices on the southern side of the Central Business District. The old mendicant's presence at the funeral had intrigued him, and he was anxious to ask her how she knew his mother. But that morning she wasn't at the intersection. Paul even parked his car on the side of the road for fifteen minutes, hoping she would return to her usual place. But she never came. That afternoon he left the office earlier than usual, but still the old woman wasn't at the intersection. The day they buried his mother there had been a few people with summer colds and Paul wondered whether she hadn't caught flue too.

Later that day, some of his workmates who had been unable to attend the funeral invited him for drinks at a noisy bar near their offices and commiserated with him in the only way they knew how – by consuming a staggering amount of alcohol, first at the bar and then at a nightclub. Hannah sent him an SMS to say she had arrived safely and resumed work. After supper he started dozing intermittently in front of the TV. He went into his bedroom and lay, fully clothed, across the width of the bed. The maid who did his housekeeping had left the window open, and a squadron of mosquitoes was soon menacingly circling him looking for blood-sucking opportunities. Disorientated by the whine of the mosquitoes, he returned to the lounge and sat in a different settee. Something flew silently across his vision. It was only a moth but it seemed so much bigger and more menacing. He tried to focus on an old black-and-white photograph of his late mother which stood on the mantelpiece. But it wasn't his mother's face; it was the wrinkled, toothless face of the old crone at the intersection.

The following day was Saturday, and Paul woke up with a terrible hangover and a text message from Lawrence saying that one of their late mother's colleagues from the women's league had written a belated but interesting obituary in *The Herald*. So, getting in his car, he quickly drove to the intersection near his flat to buy the newspaper from a vendor. The old woman he had glimpsed at the funeral was still conspicuous by her absence. He felt that something was not quite right. And he was still curious to find out how the woman knew his mother. Maybe they were distantly related, or perhaps the old lady and his mother had been in the ruling party's women's league together. He thought that perhaps Fatso, the newspaper vendor, would know something, and wondered why he has not asked before.

'Where's that old lady who usually begs for money from here?'

'Auntie Bee?'

'I don't know her name.'

'Don't you know?'

'Know what?'

'She was run over by a kombi last week.'

'That's terrible...'

'And she died right here, on that side of the road.'

'Fatso, are you serious?'

'I'm serious. She had passed long before the ambulance arrived.'

'Do you know where she lived?'

'Auntie Bee was a beggar. Nobody knows where she lived. Didn't you know who she was?'

'No. I only ever saw her here on my work way to work.'

'Auntie Bee's husband was Comrade Tikitiki Mamvemve.'

Paul remembered the man, a colleague of his late father's. Both men had been key members of the nationalist delegation at the Lancaster House conference, which had finally ended the country's brutal armed conflict. Paul remembered his father once telling him that he and Comrade Tikitiki both came from the same village and had attended the same primary and secondary schools. Years after Independence, Comrade Mamvemve had perished in a mysterious car accident but had still been declared a national hero, leading to his interment at Heroes' Acre. The President had delivered an impassioned graveside eulogy which had lasted close to an hour. As usual, His Excellency used the occasion to berate his traditional foes – the opposition party, the British prime minister, the American president, gays and lesbians.

'But Fatso, wasn't that man buried at Heroes' Acre about ten years ago?'

'Yes, he was.'

'So, how did his wife end up living rough on the streets?'

'Being the widow of a national hero means nothing. After that big funeral that was live on television people just forgot about her. Her own sons chased her away from her home and then quickly sold it. I have known those boys for years. They're wild and just do drugs, alcohol and clubs.'

Paul remembered how much he had drunk, just the night before, and the hallucinations that had followed. The memories were fresh and uncomfortable, and he brushed them aside.

'When did this accident happen?'

'About two days ago. The kombi driver didn't even stop.'

'You say she was taken to the hospital?'

'Yes. The ambulance took her to the general hospital. But like I said, she'd already passed away.'

Paul thanked him and turned back to his car. The casualty department directed him to the mortuary and there he was directed to a precast concrete shed at the back of the building. Within, a few people sat on a single wooden bench, grief mirrored on their sweaty faces. Paul sat next to a middle-aged man who smelt faintly of smoke and wondered if he'd spent the night at a wake. The mourner stared straight ahead, a distant but haunted look in his eyes. The male being served at the single desk sat ramrod still, as if his whole body had been stiffened by bereavement. The queue moved very slowly. Paul glanced through his newspaper. His mother's obituary was tucked away on an inside page, accompanied by a photograph of some members of the women's league in the early eighties. He recognised the person standing next to his mother as the woman from the intersection. After about half an hour, it was his turn. Paul cleared his throat to announce his presence.

'Yes?'

'I have been directed to this office.'

'What is the name of the deceased?'

'Well...'

'And how are you related to the deceased?'

'It's about an old lady who passed away two days ago.'

'I'm very sorry for your loss,' said the clerk, finally looking up from his mound of papers.

'I wanted to find out if I can, in some small way, contribute to the funeral expenses?'

'Was this old lady a relative of yours?'

'Well....'

'Was it the one with the missing front teeth or the one with the perforated nostrils?'

'The one with the missing front teeth...'

'She was buried early this morning.'

'Oh, I see.'

'The thing is, Mr...?'

'Chimusoro.'

'The thing is, Mr Chimusoro, we kept the deceased here for two days but nobody came forward to claim it. And, as she had no identification papers on her, we had to give her a pauper's burial as per regulations. You know, we've a limited capacity for keeping bodies here.'

'Oh, I see. Which cemetery did you bury her in?'

The man told him. It was the same one in which they had buried his mother. Dejectedly, Paul stood up and made his way to the door of the shed. The clerk gave him a cursory glance and said perfunctorily,

'I'm very sorry for your loss.'

Paul wondered how often he offered that phrase every day. Deciding to go to the cemetery, Paul bought two bouquets of flowers, one for his mother's grave, and the other for the old lady's. Arriving, an elderly attendant took him to the section with the paupers' graves. There were about a dozen fresh mounds in a neat row, but they all looked the same. Paul looked at the attendant, who was disinterestedly hand-rolling a cigarette in a piece of paper torn from an old newspaper.

'An old lady, with two front teeth missing, was buried here this morning. I want to lay a wreath. Which one is her grave?'

'Mister, these are all graves of old ladies buried this morning. My work here is only to look after the cemetery, so how would I know which one had her front teeth missing?'

The attendant spat forcefully into the red earth at his feet and walked away, mumbling incoherently under his breath. Paul walked to his mother's grave and placed the two bouquets on top of it. A previous bouquet placed there had died. He picked it up and placed it in a bin on his way out. He wondered if he would have offered more to the old lady had he known who she was. As he walked out, an inscription on a tombstone caught his eye: 'Whoever is kind to the poor lends to the Lord, because it's only the giving that makes you what you are.' Paul shook his head, as if to drive the memory away. He lived in a different world.

# 2

## The Day Morgan Died

Morgan Chamunorwa died on the same day as his namesake, Morgan Tsvangirai, the leader of the opposition party. For the previous three days, a barn owl had quietly roosted in the large *muhacha* tree that overlooked Chamunorwa's homestead. It sat on a branch with is head cocked to one side, silently following proceedings in the parched landscape below. Morgan's wife Lydia, who tended him in his final days, told her youngest sister Scholastic that an owl outside the hut of a sick man was a bad omen. Even more unusual, she added, was the sight of an owl during daytime. On St. Valentine's Day, Morgan quietly passed away on a reed mat in the main hut where he had spent his final, painful hours.

Throughout the day and the following morning, Morgan's relatives, neighbours and friends congregated at his homestead at Chinyana kraal, under Chief Mtendadzanwa, for the funeral wake. One of Morgan's elderly uncles told the mourners that he had cycled thirty-five kilometres from his village to attend the funeral. All the mourners tried to console Morgan's widow, but Lydia's grief seemed so profound that none of their tears could ease it. She told them that her husband's final wish was to be buried underneath the *muhacha* tree on the perimeter of his homestead, close to where his infant son had been buried five years previously. Scholastic also told the gathering mourners of her late brother-in-law's final wishes.

Every new arrival wanted to know the exact details of the young farmer's death. Lydia, despite her anguish, told them the same story. The previous morning, her husband had been gored by a bad-tempered bull, which he had been tethering to a plough, prior to cultivating his field. One of the bull's horns had gone straight through his shoulder, causing heavy bleeding which Lydia couldn't stop. She had been all alone with her husband, as all the other villagers had gone to the fields for the day and going to seek help would have meant leaving Morgan alone and unattended in the hut where he lay. There were no hospitals in the Chinyana area – the nearest medical facility was a small clinic at a mission school some twenty kilometres away. Lydia told mourners that she watched helplessly as her husband's life slowly ebbed away.

'Once God has decided that someone should go,' one of Lydia's aunts consoled her, 'there's nothing anybody can do.'

Morgan's four uncles who lived in a distant village – Barnabas, Douglas, Muchadeyi and Elias – arrived later in the morning. They had used a donkey-drawn scotch-cart and it had taken them three hours to get to Chinyana. After lunch, they sat down with some of Lydia's senior male relatives to discuss the burial arrangements. Before long there was a disagreement. Lydia's male relatives, on behalf of his widow, conveyed the dead man's last wish that he wanted to be buried behind his three huts in the shade of the *muhacha* tree, next to his infant son. Barnabas said that Morgan's late father, Mudzuri, their nephew, had expressed his own dying wish that his son should be buried next to him in their home village of Zhumbare. There was a stalemate.

When informed of the impasse, Lydia said she wanted to respect her husband's last wish but if his uncles were insisting on different arrangements, she would not stand in their way. She was, however, also adamant that she would not participate in their plans. When told that the idea was to take her husband's body to his father's home village, she said she would not go, and her relatives also said that they would not attend the ceremony. Undeterred, Barnabas, as the deceased man's eldest uncle, took it upon himself to make an announcement to the mourners concerning the burial programme. To ease the tension, he started with a compliment:

'In our clan we have a saying that if you want to impress visitors you cook them your fattest hen. We are very happy with the lunch we have been given here and would like to thank our daughter-in-law Lydia for having looked after our son Morgan in his final hours. She has told me of his last wish about where he wanted to be buried, but as you know, Morgan came from Zhumbare, where his father raised him. He came to this village because the government gave him a small farm under the land reform programme and he wanted to try his hand at farming. Morgan's father passed away when he was very young and we, his father's brothers, became his surrogate fathers. So, we now have the authority to make the necessary decisions concerning…'

'What about his wife, Ambuya Lydia?' Somebody shouted from the back of the seated mourners.

'Who's that fool?' asked Nelson, Morgan's uncle, the one who claimed to have cycled thirty-five kilometres to come to the funeral.

'Shapiro,' somebody replied, 'just ignore him. He's the village idiot and always makes a fool of himself at funerals.'

'Idiot or not, he's got a point. Maybe we should listen to him.'

This request, made by one of Lydia's aunts, was ignored. Barnabas continued. 'As I was saying before that interruption, we've made the decision to take our deceased son to his home village. We have arranged for a lorry to ferry the coffin and mourners there, as it is ninety kilometres away. The burial of our nephew will take place at Chinyautsa kraal tomorrow at half past two in the afternoon.'

Later that day, a carpenter hired by Barnabas brought a coffin to the hut where Chamunorwa's body had been wrapped in a blanket. Barnabas and his brothers prepared the body according to their traditional rituals. The skies were turning grey and thunder rolled in the distance. Supper was served at five, to allow the funeral cortège enough time to travel to Zhumbare. The male mourners retreated to the cleared area behind the huts, where there was a fire-pit and a drum of the potent traditional beer known as *seven days*. Some reminisced about Morgan Chamunorwa, the young tobacco farmer, who was a pillar of the village community. Others talked about Morgan Tsvangirai, the opposition leader who for many years fought the tyranny of a country brutalised by dictatorship.

'I'll try and get details of Mr Tsvangirai's funeral from my Harare contacts in the party,' said one of the mourners. 'I want to attend.'

'Me too,' said Shapiro. 'That man was one of us.'

'Yes. But I don't think they'll bury him at the Heroes' Acre.'

'If you're a true hero, it doesn't matter where you're buried,' responded Shapiro. 'The people of this country know who their true heroes are.'

By the time the hired lorry arrived, it had started to drizzle. The pallbearers carrying the coffin found that they could no longer manoeuvre it through the doorway, although they tried from all angles. Exasperated, Barnabas sat down on the cold floor and together with Muchadeyi, his youngest brother, they decided to remove the body from the coffin. This was then carried outside and placed in the casket, which had been much easier to shift when it was empty. Meantime Lydia and the other female mourners watched, wailing uncontrollably. By the time the lorry left for Zhumbare, it was dark and rain was pouring down. The dozen or so mourners accompanying the coffin at the back of the lorry had to shelter under plastic sheeting, which the driver had had the good sense to bring with him. Some of the male mourners continued drinking the *seven days*, which they had smuggled from the homestead in plastic bottles.

Less than ten kilometres into its journey, one of the lorry's rear tyres developed a puncture. For about half an hour the driver parked on the side of the road, hoping the rains would abate so he could change it. But the storm was unrelenting. Finally, Barnabas instructed that tyre be changed in the heavy downpour. The people at the back of the lorry had to dismount, to reduce the vehicle's weight as it was lifted up by the jack. The coffin had to be lifted and placed on the side of the road. In the darkness, the mourners huddled underneath a tree singing religious songs. The storm soon abated but not the wind. At last, the lorry resumed its journey. About ten kilometres further on, the vehicle had to turn onto an uneven gravel track. After another five kilometres or so, Barnabas struck a match to light his hand-rolled cigarette. In the dim glow, he briefly scanned the faces of the mourners huddled around the coffin, then suddenly called to the driver to stop.

'Where's Shapiro?'

The mourners looked at each other in dismay. Then one of them muttered,

'When we were changing the tyre, I saw him walking off into the bushes. I didn't seem him come back.'

'Maybe he was going to relieve himself. *Seven days* can really mess up your stomach...'

'So we've left him behind?'

'But we can't leave him in the middle of nowhere. We'll have to go back for him.'

The female mourners began wailing as the driver, cursing under his breath, turned the lorry around. He prayed he would have enough fuel to complete the journey. He did not need any more mishaps. By now it was almost dawn. They found Shapiro sitting underneath a tree, his exposed arms goose-pimpled by the early morning dew. Ignoring the accusative stares from the other mourners, the drunken man mumbled an apology and climbed sheepishly into the back of the lorry.

'Douglas,' said Barnabas, 'you have better eyesight than me. Look at the tree where we placed the coffin when we were changing the tyre... Isn't that the same owl that was in the *muhacha* tree at Morgan's house yesterday morning?'

'I don't know. All owls look the same to me.'

'I wonder if it's been following us,' said Barnabas.

As the mourners watched in silence, the owl flew off into the sunrise. The lorry resumed its journey. The rain had stopped. Some of the female mourners at the back of the lorry fell asleep. Everyone was cold, wet, hungry and tired. Aware of the increasingly poor road, the driver reduced the lorry's speed to a snail's pace, as a precaution. This only added to his passengers' anxieties. Those still awake soon turned their frustrations on Shapiro, whose brief disappearance they blamed for lengthening the distance to their final destination. Nelson, Morgan's uncle who had cycled thirty-five kilometres to the funeral, was not in a charitable mood.

'Shapiro, you're responsible for this long journey. Next time we will leave you alone in the middle of the bush...'

'Yes, then you can deal with the hyenas and the jackals...'

'Leave him alone, he was just answering the call of nature.'

'That's because he was drinking all day. This is a funeral and not a wedding. We should have some respect for my departed nephew.'

But Shapiro, unhappy at being pilloried, was determined to have the final word.

'All I said was that we should have listened to my *ambuya*, Lydia, and respected the dead man's final wish. Now we're going to bury him in a strange place – and *without* his widow!'

At last they reached a narrow bridge about thirty kilometres from their destination and were dismayed to discover that the storm had washed it away. Douglas, perhaps the most sober of the group, told the driver that there was a different route they could use running beside a newly-built dam. By this time, the driver was exhausted. He was also worried about fuel and wondered if he would receive any compensation for all the extra miles. He decided to bring up the subject of money with Barnabas when they reached their destination. For the moment, in order to maintain cordial relations with the bereaved, he had no choice except to follow the wishes of those who had hired him. Taking a deep breath, and stretching his tired shoulders, he restarted the engine and began to turn the vehicle around. He felt a grim sense of foreboding. He had never been responsible for a coffin on a journey that had had so many setbacks. A superstitious man, he felt that the route was being haunted by a disappointed spirit. And yet he had no choice but to continue. And, as if to confirm his worst fears, a few kilometres down the road they were stopped by two large *muhacha* trees that had fallen across the track, blocking further progress. The fallen trees had taken down some of the tall electricity pylons nearby, rendering the road not only impassable, but dangerous.

'Must have been the storm,' said Barnabas.

'Yes,' agreed Douglas.

The driver pulled over onto the side of the road. He was drained, his clothes were still wet from the rain, and he was hungry. As politely as he could, he asked Barnabas what they wanted to do, since they could no longer proceed to Zhumbare. Barnabas and Douglas discussed the issue for a while but failed to reach a decision. They moved to the back of the lorry and consulted several of the elderly mourners, who were also tired and wet. The sun had come out and some of the people at the back had disembarked to stretch their legs. An unpleasant odour had started wafting from the coffin. The female mourners were holding handkerchiefs to their noses. Shapiro, now sober, offered Barnabas and his brother a simple solution.

'I think that we should just go back and bury him where he wanted to be buried. We have to respect a dying man's wish.'

'But what about the wishes of his own father?'

'Yes, the wishes of his father are important. But in this case, I think his own wishes override those of a parent. That's the way we would do it in our clan.'

Early in the afternoon of the next day, a sizable crowd gathered underneath the *muhacha* tree at Morgan Chamunorwa's homestead. Amongst the mourners were his widow Lydia, her sister Scholastic and their relatives. Also, in attendance were Barnabas Chamunorwa, his brothers and his relatives. As the last shovel of earth was added to the mound of red earth above the grave, a giant owl, which had been roosting in the *muhacha* tree, flew away into the midday haze. The mourners watched in silence. As they began to disperse, Shapiro shook his head.

'I think people should always respect a dying person's wishes. The man said he wanted to be buried next to his son. Why were his uncles trying to force matters by taking him to a place he clearly didn't want to be?'

# 3

# *The Fall of Man*

It was known as the chameleon's tunnel, an eight kilometre pass of steep gradients and treacherous curves cutting through the red hills between Mashakada business centre and Saginaw Farm. The bends forced motorists to reduce speed to a chameleon's pace, hence the nickname given by frustrated drivers to that part of the highway.

The statutory speed limit was sixty kilometres an hour for ten kilometres on both sides of the pass, but the signs indicating this restriction had long been rendered unreadable, smeared with the graffiti of passing vandals. Most drivers, finding themselves stuck behind the haulage trucks that plied this busy but dangerous road, became impatient and routinely broke the speed limit with risky overtaking manoeuvres. The traffic police, aware of these lucrative infractions, mounted daily speed traps behind a clump of trees next to a lay-by just after the last bend.

Constable Philemon Nyakabau had been with the Zimbabwe Republic Police's traffic section for less than three years, but he had quickly learned the ropes. He was thirty-three years old and recently married. His wife was expecting their first child and he was excited at the prospect of first-time fatherhood. A devout Christian, he was often invited by the pastor of his church to give lay sermons on the evils of corruption, his country's most pervasive vice. The previous Sunday, he had spoken about the fall of man –

14

how Adam's capitulation to temptation condemned mankind to eternal damnation. Impressed by his zeal, the pastor of the Zionist Lutheran Assembly invited him to give another sermon during the Christmas Day service the following week.

Philemon already knew from experience that the festive season was the best time for the traffic police to make money. On his days off, he would team up with two colleagues, Atherton Mbizi and Norman Sibanda, and place speed traps near the chameleon's tunnel lay-by. Most motorists grudgingly paid the spot fines, so they could continue with their journeys. Alternatively, recalcitrant drivers were told they were free to contest the accuracy of the alleged speed by having their day in court. However, during the second week in December, there had been continuous rain and the team failed to achieve its targets. Their favourite *modus operandi* was a simple ambush – hiding in the undergrowth or behind trees and springing into view at the last minute. But their bright green sleeves made them fairly easy to spot and when it was raining motorists would speed past them as they sheltered under trees. The drivers would then warn oncoming traffic by flashing their headlights. As the constables dejectedly made their way back to the police station that Friday, Philemon Nyakabau had intriguing news for his younger compatriots.

'Do you guys really want to know what happens to the spot fines we collect?'

'The money goes to treasury.'

'No, I was told it goes towards a special medical fund set up to help policemen injured in the line of duty.'

'Gentlemen, you're both wrong.'

'Okay. What do you want to tell us?'

'Three quarters of the money we collect goes towards building the Commissioner-General's house.'

'The C-G? Our boss?'

'Yes.'

'I think I read something about that on WhatsApp, but I dismissed it as fake news.'

'It's not fake news, *mukoma*. I've been to that house. It's huge! It's almost as big as the president's house in Borrowdale. It's got a swimming pool, Jacuzzi, sauna, tennis court and an entertainment gazebo. The garage accommodates six vehicles and the perimeter walls around the stand are as high as those at the Remand Prison. I tell you, *mukoma*, if you went there you'd think you were in Dubai, New York, Cape Town or London – except that nobody else builds walls as high as ours.'

'Where's this house?'

'It's in Glen Lorne, in that new area where all our top bosses gave themselves stands – Police Heights...'

'Are you serious, Philemon?'

'I swear, on my grandmother's grave. The size of that house made me want to cry with anger. Most houses in that area are owned by our senior officers. And you should ask yourself how they manage to build such huge marble palaces on their paltry salaries...'

'You mean, we're standing in the rain collecting money for the *chefs* to spend....'

'It's daylight robbery.'

'Exactly...'

'So, Philemon, what do you have in mind?'

'It's simple. We're given our daily targets. If we start early, we will have met them by midday. After that, everything we collect is ours and we split it three ways. The big boss gets to build his Glen Lorne mansion, and we buy ourselves small stands in the high density areas. This way, everyone gets something.'

\*\*\*

Two days before Christmas, the constables devised a plan to guarantee that they would collect enough fines to ensure their festive season, just like their superiors', was also memorable. To avoid surprise visits by their bosses, the three policemen agreed that the extra money would be kept in a supermarket bag hidden behind a tree. Philemon assigned the day's duties. Atherton would hide behind a tree on the last bend, and as a speeding motorist went past, he would make a hand signal to Norman, who in turn would alert Philemon so he could be ready with his speed gun. The device didn't work, but the motorists didn't know that. Most were intimidated into compliance by the sight of traffic policemen standing menacingly on the edge of the highway, and by their aggressive denials of any refutation.

Anyone who dared to argue would be shown a number on the screen of the speed gun, indicating their vehicle's alleged illegal speed. After the driver had paid the spot fine, he would be issued with an 'admission of guilt' receipt. Philemon, as always, was to be the last line of defence. Hiding behind a large baobab tree next to the lay-by, he would await Norman's hand signal before throwing a spiked metal bar underneath the front wheels of any non-compliant vehicles. This crude device was standard issue for the traffic police, and Philemon had hired a welder to fabricate his bar to his own specification. Throwing it was a dangerous exercise that required impeccable timing, guile and lightning-fast reflexes. But the end reward made the risk worthwhile. And Philemon, a decent hurdler during his secondary school days, was always more than equal to the task.

Another mandatory accessory of the traffic police's destructive armoury was a metal-studded baton, known colloquially as *mbhoma*, used to smash the windscreens of non-compliant commuter kombis in order to obstruct the driver's view. Inevitably, some drivers would lose control of their vehicles, concluding their lives in a fatal accident. Despite frequent public outcries about the heavy-handedness, the use of excessive force and police extortion, the authorities turned a blind eye. Sometimes, after a terrible tragedy, the national police spokeswoman would appear on state-controlled television saying the full wrath of the law would be unleashed on those motorists caught flouting the rules of the road. The Commissioner-General of police never blamed his officers, despite ample evidence that most of the serious traffic incidents were initiated by his overzealous and under-paid officers who were threatened with dismissal if they did not bring in the income their bosses demanded. The traffic police and the kombi drivers had become mortal enemies, daily playing a dangerous game in which each tried to outwit the other in a vicious war of attrition.

\*\*\*

It's just after quarter to one in the afternoon. On the other side of the chameleon's tunnel, Obert Mhofu, an unemployed UZ graduate, is driving back to Harare from the southern border town of Beitbridge. He's alone, happy, and looking forward to the Christmas holiday. Two days earlier, he had hitch-hiked to the border to collect his new Japanese import, a Toyota Spacio, which he intends to use as an unregistered taxi – a *mshikashika* – on the streets of Harare's chaotic central business district. The vehicle cost him three thousand dollars, money he borrowed from relatives and saved from temporary jobs. The car is not exactly new, as it is a 2010 model with ninety-five thousand kilometres on the clock. Three years after leaving college, Obert has been unable to secure gainful employment to enable him to look after his wife and three-year old son. Like most people of his age, he has dispatched his CV far and wide, but it seems nobody is interested in the services of a bilingual social scientist with a lower-second degree.

It was an old friend from his college days, Tawanda, who advised Obert to go into the *mshikashika* business. Also an unemployed graduate, Tawanda had managed to put together enough money to purchase a Japanese import the previous year. He seemed to have done well enough to acquire a residential stand in a medium density suburb on the outskirts of the city. Tawanda had given some salutary advice to Obert on how to survive in the cut-and-thrust business of unregistered taxis. First and foremost, he warned Obert, it was essential to maintain a cordial relationship with the traffic police, especially the junior officers. He also told Obert to expect to spend between thirty and forty per cent of his daily earnings on two obligatory expenses – fuel and 'toll gate' fees, the latter being bribes paid daily to certain traffic policemen.

'You have to pay the toll gate fees, otherwise the cops will harass you all day and you won't make any money. The traffic cops are not your friends, but the last thing you want is for them to be your enemy.'

As he approaches the first bend into the chameleon's tunnel, Obert notices that the traffic ahead of him has slowed down. The reason for this is soon apparent. Two trans-border haulage trucks, known as *gonyets*, are tortuously winding their way through the second bend, spewing black exhaust fumes into the air and causing the dozen or so cars behind them to slow right down. Obert, eager to get home and show his wife his new vehicle, silently curses the *gonyets* and increases the volume of the car radio in frustration. He knows the eight-kilometre drive through the bends is going to be a long one. Then a hundred-metre stretch of straight road suddenly opens up ahead of him, giving him an opportunity to overtake the three pick-up trucks in front of him. He tucks himself behind an over-loaded commuter kombi in the nick of time. Pleased with himself, he sings along to a tune on the radio.

On the other side of the chameleon's tunnel, Philemon, Norman and Atherton have been in position for over five hours. They have already fined half a dozen drivers for speeding, amassing three hundred dollars in the process. Philemon has fined three motorists twenty dollars each for not having spare wheels, a bus driver has been fined fifteen dollars for allowing a passenger to throw an empty Castle lager can out of a window and a fearful elderly woman has been fined thirty dollars for having a broken tail-light and a fire extinguisher with the wrong specifications. By lunchtime, the daily target had been met. The men were now collecting money to be shared amongst themselves at the end of the day, putting it in their well-hidden supermarket bag.

Just after one o'clock, Atherton sees the two *gonyets* approaching the last bend and his heart sinks. Just like the motorists, the traffic police don't like *gonyets*. These unwieldy juggernauts slow down the traffic behind them, diminishing the prospects of catching over-speeding vehicles. But today Atherton is in luck. As the leading *gonyet's* muzzle nudges the crest of the tunnel, Obert Mhofu's silver

Toyota Spacio appears on the horizon, overtaking the four vehicles behind the two huge trucks with breathtaking speed regardless of the danger to himself and others. Atherton realises the vehicle is new, as it does not have registration plates. Then a sudden downpour forces him to duck under a tree. He now has no way of alerting Norman of the offending vehicle's imminent approach.

The shower is heavy and the surface of the road very slippery. Obert, who is concentrating on passing the leading *gonyet,* which has almost ground to a halt on the crest of the final hill, doesn't notice Atherton Mbizi crouched behind a tree. And because he's still singing along to Jah Prayzah, he also fails to notice Norman Sibanda making a frantic hand signal to Philemon Nyakabau, who is hiding next to the lay-by, *mbhoma* and spiked metal bar at the ready. Caught unawares by the car's speed, Norman scrambles up a ridge, so he can alert Philemon who is further down the road. But because of the rain, visibility is poor and Norman is unable to see his colleague. With a final accelerated flourish, Obert grits his teeth and eases past the *gonyet* just after the final bend.

The sudden appearance of a car around the final bend catches Philemon by surprise. His experience tell him the Spacio must be doing close to eighty kilometres an hour, and he wonders why Norman has not given him the usual signal. He decides to stop the car and tell the driver he was doing seventy kilometres an hour in a sixty kilometre zone. He knows it will be his word against the driver's, but a traffic policeman's word always carries the day. He steps onto the edge of the road, one hand waving the vehicle to stop whilst the other wields the spiked metal bar. At that moment, the rain changes direction, momentarily blurring his vision. The Spacio is approaching fast, and Philemon can see it won't stop. He has no option but to throw the metal bar and get out of the way. As the bar slides across the wet tarmac, Obert swerves violently to avoid the obstacle, and heads straight for Philemon. Leaping out of harm's way, the policeman jumps over a roadside ditch to the safety of a grassy verge. But he loses his balance, skids in the rain, and lands buttocks first on the upturned metal bar at the bottom of the ditch. The Spacio wheezes past in a blur of water and exhaust fumes.

\*\*\*

On the day he was admitted to Harare Hospital, Philemon Nyakabau was given an anti-tetanus injection and strong pain-killers. A nurse kept him under constant observation, monitoring his blood pressure. Then two young doctors spent close to an hour stitching up his badly lacerated buttocks. His anal canal had been partially blocked by internal bleeding and it had been necessary to attach a colostomy bag to the area just above his pelvic bone, to relieve his bowels. One of the young doctors told Philemon he had been very lucky as a spike had missed his testicles by a hair's breath.

The following morning, Constable Philemon Nyakabau was discharged from hospital. The doctor told him his injuries were not life threatening and gave him some antibiotics and analgesics to take at home. As he lay in bed nursing his sore buttocks, a news item tucked on an inside page of a state-controlled newspaper caught his attention. In its daily compilation of the festive season's road accidents, the paper reported that an off-duty traffic policeman on his way home had been knocked down by a speeding vehicle on the Harare-Beitbridge highway.

'The policeman in question is now recovering at home,' the paper quoted the police spokeswoman as saying. 'We believe a drunk driver was behind the hit-and-run and follow-up inquiries are currently in progress. However, we strongly urge motorists not to drink and drive during this festive period. As per our mandate, the full wrath of the law will be unleashed on those caught flouting the rules of the road...'

Philemon's colleagues, Norman Sibanda and Atherton Mbizi, visited him at home later that day. They brought a basket of assorted fruit and a get-well card from the traffic section. When they were leaving, they told Philemon that their immediate superior had demanded a full report of what had happened at the chameleon's tunnel, including a detailed explanation why three off-duty traffic officers were manning an unauthorised speed-trap in an area three hundred kilometres outside their jurisdiction. It was the day before Christmas, and Philemon suddenly remembered he needed to work on the sermon that he was supposed to give the following day to the expectant congregants of the Zionist Lutheran Assembly – the fall of man.

# 4

# Hallelujah Kingdom

*The demons begged Jesus: 'If you drive us out, send us into a herd of pigs.'*
Matthew 8:31

Things started going badly for Augustine Nhembe in the winter of 2015. Golden Homes Realty, the real estate company for which he worked, advised staff through an internal memo there had been a huge drop in the sale of residential properties due to factors beyond its control. There were to be mandatory redundancies across all departments. Having been with the company for less than two years, Augustine knew his future was uncertain. Also, because he had been a part-time negotiator whose remuneration was commission-based, he knew he would not be entitled to the statutory three months' salary payable to those laid off without notice.

Augustine worked part-time at Golden Homes because he had other commitments. For two days a week, he was employed by the correctional services to give religious instruction to male prisoners at Chikurubi Prison. It was voluntary work, but they paid him enough to cover his direct expenses. He was brought up in a strict Christian household and always wanted to help others, especially those disadvantaged by the circumstances of their upbringing. His father was a staunch Catholic who sent all his five children to decent boarding schools. Augustine remembered his father as a dedicated opponent of science who always entered into arguments with his more educated but less spiritually enlightened relatives.

In his mid-twenties, Augustine married his high school sweetheart, Ernestina. Within three years the couple had two young daughters, Rumbidzai and Chiedza, and were looking forward to having more children. The Book of Genesis urged man to go forth and increase in number, and Augustine and Ernestina were determined to fulfil God's wishes. However, Augustine's life of simple contentment came to an abrupt end when he found himself jobless in a country with a collapsed economy. The prospects of an upturn in the real estate industry were dim, and Augustine knew he would have to find other ways to survive.

Month by month, he struggled to make ends meet. The two girls attended primary school, the rent for his three-room lodgings needed to be paid and there were other bills that needed to be settled regularly. His engagement with the correctional services was sporadic, and the family had to rely on his wife's irregular income from the second-hand clothes her two employees sold from a stall at a city flea market. Most of the business ventures Augustine attempted, undertaken more in hope than conviction, flopped dismally. One day, as he sat gloomily in the bedroom of his rented cottage, an idea took shape in his mind. He soon concluded that if handled properly, it would put an end to his earthly tribulations, and provide a secure future for his young family.

Augustine decided to become a prophet, a man of God. He knew he would need luck to succeed in the congested business of commercial prophecy. But he was optimistic, having learnt from his father that luck was nothing more than opportunity and preparation. On television, he would watch in admiration as West African men of God filled stadiums and performed mind-blowing miracles. The newspapers were full of stories about this new breed of gospel entrepreneurs, men who used the Bible as a bridge to attain worldly comforts. One such new crusader held weekly gatherings in a soccer stadium attended by hundreds of devotees, including high-profile politicians and socialites. Another man of God was rumoured to own vast tracts of prime residential land and a fleet of imported vehicles. Augustine was determined to be the latest addition to this brood of youthful God-promoting tycoons.

One Sunday morning, he invited some of his neighbours to the back of his landlord's house and preached the word of God. He told them that the Lord had told him in a dream what was wrong with the country and how it could be corrected. He was an eloquent, persuasive speaker and those in attendance listened attentively, even though they did not always agree with him. Unfortunately, his landlord also did not agree with some of his lodger's political views and soon asked him to move his Sunday church services elsewhere, as he would be left with no other option other than to evict him. Undeterred, Augustine found a disused cinema in the city centre and moved his church to these premises. He called his church 'God's Grace Ministries', and in front of the building he placed an illuminated billboard that read: '*Welcome to the Hallelujah Kingdom*'. Soon, the church was attracting more than a hundred people to its main Sunday service, including several cabinet ministers and their spouses.

He became known as Prophet Augustine, and his wife became Prophetess Ernestina. The church welcomed everybody through its doors – the homeless, the bereaved, those in financial straits and other lost souls who survived on the fringes of an ambivalent society. As someone who grew up in the church, Augustine knew how to preach the gospel of love, good neighbourliness and tolerance. He told the congregants that faith was an integral part of the new ministry, and abstinence and humility would be its paramount virtues. He told them that the pure life they sought was at their fingertips and, if they had faith in him, the eternal life they yearned for would no longer be a distant nirvana. Within five months of its existence, the new ministry was receiving generous donations from its congregants, money which Augustine said would go towards the construction of a new church building on a piece of ground donated by one of the government ministers who was a congregant.

After two months, Augustine was able to vacate his cramped lodgings in Highfield and move to a more spacious, double-storey, four-bedroom house in Meyrick Park. The house came with a swimming pool, solar power, a maid and a gardener. At weekends, Augustine and Ernestina held *braais* for their congregants while the children frolicked in the sparkling waters of the pool. People kept flocking to the Sunday services, and Augustine was soon invited to be a panellist on a popular religious radio programme. He spent days preparing for the event, because he knew the free publicity that went with it was an opportunity he could ill afford to miss. Because of his gift of oratory, he easily outshone the other panellists and was invited to host his own Sunday evening radio programme. The more his fame and popularity grew, the more new converts his ministry attracted.

Mabel Gumbo and her childhood friend, Nancy Khumalo, were amongst the ministry's new recruits. Both were in their late-seventies and suffered from the usual conditions associated with the ageing process. Mrs Gumbo had rheumatoid arthritis, high blood pressure and diabetes. Mrs Khumalo suffered from acute lumbago, chronic osteoporosis and mild Parkinson's. Both women were obese, a handicap that caused them great discomfort and restricted their mobility. Five years earlier, they belonged to a ministry headed by a prophet who had promised that he would cure their troublesome conditions. But after spending fortunes on the prophet's anointing oils and miracle soaps, both of them had realised perhaps it was time to move on. Soon afterwards, a sleazy tabloid exposed the prophet as an accomplished fraudster who had once been convicted for masterminding a usurious credit facility. He also sold a mythical ointment he claimed was a panacea for all known human ailments. Laboratory tests later found his miracle ointment to be a mixture of horse urine, brake fluid and anti-freeze.

Every Sunday, Mrs Gumbo and Mrs Khumalo attended

Prophet Augustine's services. They sat next to each other in the front row, where they had enough space in front of them to stretch their rheumaticky legs. They vigorously nodded their grey heads as they listened appreciatively to the uplifting sermons of this eloquent, enigmatic preacher. Every Sunday, the prophet told his congregants to shun the temptations of the flesh, because an affinity for the Devil's pleasures amounted to nothing more than spiritual desecration. People needed to share their earthly wealth with God, he would tell them. And because he was God's representative on earth, he would willingly accept all donations in cash and kind. The money thus collected, he told them, would find its way to God through the new building the church would start constructing soon. Money was bad for man, he would preach, but it was good for God. To emphasise his point, he would often conclude with a verse from the Book of Timothy:

*'For the love of money is a root of all kinds of evil...'*

The ministry's rapid growth surprised even its most cynical opponents. Prophet Augustine started appearing on television, claiming to perform miracles and exorcise evil spirits. He claimed he could make the bedridden walk and he could make the dumb talk. He held demonstrations where cripples walked and the blind regained their sight. He was scathing of his fellow prophets, whom he accused of fleecing the public through outmoded pagan rituals. He started inviting the press to his services to witness how a true man of God purified the souls of the damned through the miracle of Christian prayer. People went on television programmes and praised the new prophet who could cast out demons, just as Jesus did in the Bible. The Sunday service congregation increased threefold. Prophet Augustine knew he had to move to larger premises. He decided to find suitable land and start the construction of his own church without further delay.

One of the church's political bigwigs, a cabinet minister, managed to persuade the First Lady to take a break from her hectic schedule to be the guest of honour at the new church's ground-breaking ceremony. She agreed and spoke highly of the church's founder, praising the various humanitarian projects undertaken by God's Grace Ministries. She concluded her address by promising to be the guest of honour at the building's official opening, earmarked for later in the year. At the end of October, the building was complete. On the day of its official opening, two huge marquees were erected in the church's car park. One was reserved for the VIPs and the other for ordinary congregants. A catering company was hired to provide refreshments during the morning's programme, as well as a finger-lunch for the guests.

Congregants eagerly awaited the day of the official opening. A bandstand was erected in the space between the two marquees to accommodate a gospel band hired to entertain the guests before the First Lady's arrival. A group of female congregants lined the newly resurfaced road leading to the building. They were under instruction to ululate as soon as the motorcade came into view. A few people sat on the red-leather sofas in the VIP tent, sipping fizzy drinks and perusing the day's programme. A huge portrait of the First Lady formed the backdrop of the tent. As the morning progressed, the church's political bigwigs were conspicuously absent while the ordinary congregants seemed apprehensive. Speaking in hushed voices, they discussed the as yet unverified news that a military coup d'état had taken place overnight, and shared developments on their cellphones.

Whenever the sound of a car was heard, the atmosphere in the tents buzzed with expectation. But after several hours, anticipation turned into restlessness. Rumours swirled that whatever had happened had resulted in the president and his wife being placed under house arrest by the state's military commanders. Mrs Mabel Gumbo and Mrs Nancy Khumalo sat at the back of the second marquee, using their hands as fans to dissipate the mounting heat. As it became clear that the event would not go ahead due to the First Lady's unavailability, the faithful started streaming away in a mute procession. Mrs Gumbo and Mrs Khumalo, unwilling to move in the mid-morning heat, stubbornly remained seated. They too had heard the rumours, but such was their hope of a healing miracle that they defiantly refused to believe them.

However, after several hours of hope and denial, they began to show their frustration.

'I wonder where the prophet is,' said Mrs Khumalo for the fourth time, but with an impatient edge to her voice.

'I believe he's in his car at the intersection, waiting to accompany the First Lady's motorcade whenever it shows up. He has to be at the front of the procession.'

'And where is Prophetess Ernestina?'

'She's with him.'

'All this waiting in this heat is killing me. First of all, the prophet told us the First Lady was coming, and she isn't here. I only came because I wanted to meet her.'

'You know what? If our prophet cannot prophecy something as important as this coup thing, I don't think he's much of a prophet.'

'I agree. I'm just hoping they'll quickly finish their coup, maybe before lunchtime, and then the First Lady can come and officially open the church.'

'I have my doubts. If it's at State House, there'll be lots of food and drink. And you know how these government people like everything for free...'

After sitting in the tent longer than almost anyone else, the two women decided enough was enough. They would return to their homes in the township and play with their grandchildren. Slowly and painfully they got up from the plastic chairs, and started hobbling towards a bus shelter on an adjacent road. They ambled along in the sweltering heat, moving as fast as their cumbersome bodies would allow them.

'If we meet the First Lady's motorcade on the way, we'll wave at her.'

'Yes, mother of Tabitha. She's a true mother of the nation, and I'm sure she'll wave back.'

# 5

# *Crossroads*

The bus finally left the long distance terminus shortly before five in the evening. It was bound for a business centre deep in the Mashangara communal lands. It had not been able to meet its scheduled departure time due to mechanical problems that had eventually required the attention of a mechanic dispatched from the bus company's main depot. It was Sunday evening, and the passengers were anxious to return to their villages to begin their working week. Amongst them were about a dozen female vendors who had come to the city to sell their assorted produce at the main vegetable market.

Also on board were some weekly boarders from St Philip's secondary school, teenagers who had been home for the weekend. The rear seats were occupied by several men who lived in the village but had been to the city to indulge in a weekend of mischief. They were drinking beer and sharing a single bottle of cheap brandy while they discussed who was the better soccer player – Christiano Ronaldo or Lionel Messi? Loud and combative, each one of them had an entrenched position from which they were unwilling to budge.

Slowly, the bus moved through the sprawling disorderly town and out onto the road heading east. It was a warm winter evening and the bus driver, a bespectacled man in his mid-twenties, kept his eyes firmly on the winding, potholed road ahead. Apart from the bus's mechanical problems, the men occupying the rear seats also made him apprehensive. A devout Christian who didn't touch alcohol, he hated drunken passengers. He remembered how alcohol had transformed his father from a gentle family man into a monster prone to violent moods swings. On his previous route he had been involved in a skirmish with a group of drunken passengers. His boss accepted his apology and let him off with a warning, but reassigned him to the unpopular rural route as punishment.

After another thirty minutes, the bus briefly stopped to drop some passengers at a lay-by, which was littered with the debris of previous visitors – empty soft drink cans, peanut shells and bright chocolate wrappers. Two of the female vendors who sat at the front of the bus were complaining loudly about the shocking rise in the price of basic commodities – sugar, bread, salt, maize meal – products that gave rise to incurable conditions like diabetes and high-blood pressure, but which they still couldn't live without. The weekly boarders from St Philip's were busy on their cellphones, playing games or reading WhatsApp messages.

An hour or so afterwards, some of the drunks at the back started shouting for an emergency recess. The driver politely replied that he would stop when it was convenient, and a few minutes later, he pulled the bus into a lay-by. Several of the male passengers rushed to relieve themselves in the nearby bushes. When everybody was back on board, the driver couldn't start the vehicle. The loquacious drunks were not impressed, though it was they who had insisted that the driver stop.

'Why did you switch off the engine, when you know the bus has problems starting? Look how late we were to leave Harare.'

The driver under attack tried to explain that the mechanic had assured him there would be no more problems. His response was met with dismissive laughter. The driver disembarked to look at the engine. He was not a mechanic, but in this hostile atmosphere he had to be seen to do something. Maybe there was a problem with the diesel, which the bus company regularly bought from the black market, to cut costs.

'You think you can solve the problem,' shouted one of the drunks belligerently. 'There's nothing you can do if there's water in the diesel.'

'I know this young man,' said another drunk, 'he's a *chinja*.'

The driver, having just been labelled an opposition party supporter, ignored the baiting. Then one of the female vendors stood up and walked towards the men at the back of the bus. Hands on her hips, she admonished the intoxicated group.

'What's wrong with you people? If you can't handle alcohol, then don't drink it. So what if he supports the MDC? You, Lancelot Mangwiro! Can't you see the driver is only a young man and that he's trying his best to get us all home? Are you not ashamed of your behaviour in front of us women and all these school children? I'll tell your wife what you've been up to when I see her tomorrow.'

The woman walked sternly back to her seat to a chorus of approving ululations, as the driver opened the bonnet. One of the weekly boarders trying to help was using his cellphone torch to enable the driver to manoeuvre his hands around the cramped engine compartment. Ten minutes later, to his great relief, the driver was able to re-start the bus. As the engine roared into life, the back-seat drunks cheered and started singing a traditional song about a poor man with two cows and five troublesome donkeys. After travelling another thirty kilometres or so, the drunks requested another emergency recess, pleading that the call of nature was once again too strong for them to ignore. This time the young driver flatly refused to stop, arguing that because of the lengthy delays, he needed to make up for lost time. Lancelot Mangwiro was not impressed.

'You MDC people from the city must think all villagers are idiots. So do you want us to relieve ourselves right here where we're seated?'

'I didn't say that. There's another lay-by after the rail crossing, near the grinding mill. I can stop there.'

The rail crossing, a notorious accident black spot, was about five kilometres further on. Six months earlier, a goods train had collided with a haulage truck, killing all the four people in the vehicle. The previous year, a bus carrying devotees coming from an all-night prayer meeting had collided with an overloaded passenger train. Dozens of people had been killed, and many others injured. So great had been the loss of life, the government had been forced to declare the tragedy a national disaster.

It was now dark and windy, and a few of the passengers at the front had dozed off, sedated into inactivity by the oppressive warmth inside the vehicle. Some of the weekly boarders, struggling to suppress their giggles, were listening to the nonsensical conversations of Lancelot and his inebriated friends. Others were discreetly using their phones to take pictures and videos of the men's drunken antics. It was around that time that a goods train normally passed the rail crossing, heading south. However, the signalling system at the rail crossing had long been vandalised for its copper components, so bus drivers and motorists had to rely on good eyes, good ears and instinct.

About half a kilometre from the rail crossing, the driver slowed down, a precautionary measure that he had been drilled to observe whenever he approached a rail crossing. It was only his second trip on this particular route, and he wanted to ensure that he followed all the company instructions. A more experienced driver had warned him that sometimes inspectors would covertly board buses pretending to be passengers in order to monitor if the drivers were observing the stringent safety rules.

As he slowed down, the driver anxiously listened for sound of the goods train, because he couldn't see much in the murky darkness, and a wintry fog had ascended from the valley below, reducing visibility to less than thirty yards. The conversations in the bus became strangely subdued, interrupted by nervous coughs and drunken hiccups. Noticing both the silence and the bus's loss of speed, Lancelot Mangwiro rose groggily to his feet. As a frequent traveller who knew the route well, he felt he had the right to challenge the driver.

'Why are you slowing down?'

'Is there another problem with the engine?' another drunk shouted querulously.

'We're approaching the rail crossing. The signals don't work, so I have to be cautious,' said the driver.

'I think you're taking us for granted, young man. Some of us want to get home early, so we can find Togara's bottle store still open. You can join us there if you want.'

The driver ignored him.

'The sign on the back of the bus says that drivers are instructed to stop at all rail crossings. And that's what I intend to do.'

'That sign was put there by someone who wants to make money by using poor people like you to drive their un-roadworthy buses.'

'That may be so, Sir. But I always follow the instructions given to me by my superiors. I have a young family to look after and I want to keep my job.'

'How dare you call driving this ancient thing a job? The election is only a few days away, and we will make sure we remove you MDC people from this country for good, just like we removed Mugabe...'

'Mangwiro!' interjected the female vendor who knew Lancelot's wife, 'I think that's quite enough.'

The driver vaguely made out the train's blurred silhouette, its black muzzle effortlessly parting the fog. He couldn't tell exactly how far away it was but decided to err on the side of caution, a decision he knew would be unpopular. But he opted for the worst-case scenario for the sake of his life and the lives of the seventy-plus passengers he was carrying. He abruptly stopped the bus a few yards from the rail tracks, to loud jeers of protest from Lancelot and his unruly friends.

'Why are you now stopping in the middle of nowhere?'

'Lancelot, you and your friends must leave the driver alone. He's told us he's not crossing until the train passes. He is just doing his job.'

'He's just a coward.'

For the second time in six months, the young driver had once again been provoked by drunken passengers to the point of no return. Unable to bear the goading from Lancelot and his friends any longer, he engaged first gear and the bus started to move forward.

Then, with the bus across the tracks except for the rear wheels, the tired engine spluttered and died with a terminal click. Realising the train was barely twenty yards away, some of the passengers began to scream, frantically scrambling towards the safety of the front seats.

Moments later, the chassis of the old bus shook and rattled as the goods train struck it a glancing blow to its rear. The impact spun the bus around several times. Still upright, it ended up against a tree on the grassy verge of the road. With the loss of power the lights inside the bus went out, leaving only the ghostly radiance of cellphone screens.

One of the young students coughed nervously. The talkative vendor, breathing heavily, impatiently waved away a night insect buzzing in front of her face. The young driver wiped the sweat off his brow with an open palm, and then blew his cheeks. An overweight woman seated on one of the front seats sat wide-eyed, clutching her chest. Then Lancelot Mangwiro thrust his head out of a window and retched. The talkative female vendor shook her head. 'So, if we'd all died in this old bus, you *maZANU* would have blamed the accident on the driver because he's MDC or on sanctions. That's your problem, you can never accept responsibility.' She cast disdainful glance in the direction of Lancelot, who had slumped back in his seat.

# 6

# Providence

*The object of war is not to die for your country,
but to make the other bastard die for his.*

General George Patton

It was a wet Friday in the middle of November. Early that morning, and as usual, Yuri Mwenda boarded a *kombi* at the Warren Park rank leaving for the city centre. He was due to write his final History paper and wanted to be in good time at the university. There had been a military coup two days earlier, and small groups of soldiers were at the major city centre intersections. Some sat on top of armoured vehicles whilst others stood still in the intermittent drizzle, like numbed creatures. He knew that these men, although they chatted politely with passing pedestrians, were only following orders. The soldiers reminded him of his late grandfather, a former soldier who had taken part in Hitler's war.

From about the age of ten, Yuri lived with his grandfather. His parents had divorced but both had remarried. It was decided that to avoid friction in either new coupling, Yuri and his two siblings would be raised by their grandfather. He was very close to the old man who wrote to him regularly at his primary boarding school, which was in a remote part of the country. The cursive was unsteady and sometimes unreadable, but Yuri appreciated the effort that had gone into crafting each letter, the dried drops of candle wax that told him of his grandfather's long nights of concern about his grandson's isolated school on the eastern border, where war never seemed far off.

Yuri owned an old tin helmet, in which he kept all his most treasured possessions. It had been given to him after his grandfather's funeral on the day when they shared out the deceased person's earthly possessions. His grandfather had lived a full life, passing away peacefully in his sleep just short of his eighty-seventh year. Yuri had kept the helmet hoping it would bring him the same good fortune that it had brought his grandfather. The story of why this was so is a strange one.

\*\*\*

The Patel Brothers made Yuri's grandfather's first bespoke suit in 1946, after he returned from Hitler's war. Edison Mwenda had been discharged from the army having been badly injured in the leg while fighting for the Empire in the jungles of Malaya and Burma. His regiment was called the Central African Rifles and was made up of native auxiliary forces drawn from Britain's sub-Saharan colonies. Because of his excellent tracking skills, he was deployed in the Chin Hills of northern Burma as part of a long-range jungle penetration patrol. After rebuffing the enemy's advances, the men were moved to the east of the country, to fight the more menacing Japanese incursions near the Laotian border. When Yuri asked his grandfather why he had fought in this war, so far from home, he was always given the same answer, 'I was fighting for the King'.

Leaving for a war among strangers was the first time his grandfather had ever left the country of his birth. The young, barefoot conscripts departed on a ship from the South African port of Durban in 1943, the same year Hitler suffered a major reverse in the icy Russian winter. Edison told his teenage wife that the voyage across the sea would take six weeks, by which time he was sure the fighting would be over. His reference point was the ancient tribal skirmishes fought by the chiefs in the rural areas, which usually lasted about an hour and resulted in no serious casualties on either side. As it turned out, he was gone for nearly two years and the war itself lasted nearly six. Edison was only twenty-one at the time, but he so distinguished himself during that Burmese campaign that he was thrice mentioned in dispatches. He bought that first made-to-measure suit from the Patel Brothers with some of the money he was given as part of his disability pension.

The rest of the pension would trickle into his post office account over several years, taking three of his children – including Yuri's mother Dorothy – through primary and secondary education. The injury to his leg had been caused by heavy Japanese artillery as he tried to rescue a colleague trapped behind enemy lines. He had been awarded a bravery medal for his heroics, a flat silver disc embossed with a portrait of King George on one side. With typical modesty, he brushed aside admiration for his actions, saying that all his colleagues would have done the same had they been in his situation. 'In war men fight for each other and if necessary, they will die for each other,' he always told them.

When he returned, Edison's view of the white man had dramatically changed. In the teeming jungles of Asia, he had fought alongside white soldiers and had seen them fall in battle. He had seen them bleed and he had seen them die. He had seen that their blood was the same colour as his and that their flesh was the same texture as his. He knew that the white man was not invincible; he knew that they were not earthly gods. Returning home, he claimed that 'White people must allow us to have a voice in the affairs of the country of our birth.'

Mohammed, the elder of the two Patel brothers, was a short balding man whose garrulous vanity was only matched by the swaggering arrogance of his younger brother, the rotund, chain-smoking Ravi. There had been a third Patel brother, Omar, but he became involved in the messy post-Federation African nationalist politics and ended up being deported. His crime was to clandestinely provide funding to the nationalists and sometimes allow secret meetings to be held at his house at night. The two Indian tailors were well known in the African townships through their weekly full-page newspaper advertisements that always included the tagline: 'Outfitters to Distinguished African Gentlemen since Time Immemorial'. Enticed, affluent Africans flocked to the Patel Brothers' premises to be kitted out in the latest imported suits. Mohammed Patel died in a car accident in 1963 and although Ravi stoically persevered on his own for a couple of years, he found the going tough without the inspirational guidance of his late brother. He reluctantly closed the shop and returned to his native Goa in 1970.

Edison Mwenda would wear that cherished first suit to boxing and wrestling matches at the Mai Musodzi Hall, the social epicentre for outgoing Africans in the 1950s. In those days, men in suits were respected and admired. Suits did not come cheap, and it was common knowledge that only those in well-paid jobs could afford them. Yuri's grandmother, who abhorred blood sports, would dutifully tag along to the hall and yawn her way through the marathon bouts. In those days township boxing was not as strictly regulated as it would be in later years, and fights lasted for as long as both pugilists remained on their feet. Wrestling was a different matter altogether. A decisive half Nelson administered by a bigger opponent usually ended most contests in no time. 'You see what Hitler's War did to him?' Yuri's grandmother would often remark, as if having long-fathomed the reason behind her husband's affinity for blood sports.

But she seemed to have resigned herself to the fact that perhaps exposure to controlled violence was just the purgative he needed to cleanse his soul of the horrors he had endured in Burma. Later, when he was in secondary school, Yuri again encountered Adolf Hitler, but this time through the pedantic tuition of Mr Abbott Rusere, the master of Modern European History: 'Hitler was able to rise to power because he was a rabble-rousing orator, a demagogue of the first order...'

Apart from that Patel Brothers suit, Edison Mwenda's other

prized possession was a dented army helmet brought back as a souvenir. This misshapen object, which aroused in Yuri and his three siblings mild curiosity during their childhood, had a remarkable history. His grandfather told Yuri that he removed the helmet from the head of a dead enemy soldier after having lost his own headgear during a fierce ground battle. The Japanese soldiers – small, dogged and fearless – were a threat to the inexperienced African soldiers. They fought to the last man and took no prisoners. They were trained not to surrender and committed suicide, or hara-kiri, rather than be taken as prisoners of war.

Five of Edison Mwenda's comrades were killed during that particular onslaught. A bullet struck the side of Edison's 'new' helmet, mildly concussing him. It was only later that he realised what a miraculous escape he had had. The bullet had penetrated the helmet but by some inexplicable law of dynamics, had exited through the back without singeing a single hair on his head. In the thick of the fight, Edison had not felt a thing. The helmet of an enemy soldier had saved him.

Sometime later, he found himself separated from his unit during another ferocious dogfight with the Japanese ground forces. Wounded and disorientated in the humid Burmese jungle, he had hidden in the thick lush undergrowth as the enemy carried out mop-up operations around him. 'When you're lost in the jungle,' he once told Yuri, 'the long nights are the worst.' He would surely have died had he not had the presence of mind to plug the two bullet holes in the helmet and use it as a bucket to collect the rainwater that dripped off the succulent vegetation around him. He supplemented this meagre diet by digging up shoots, trapping small rodents and birds and chewing strips of bark. A search party found him two weeks later. And that was the second occasion when the Japanese helmet had saved his life.

'Although I was lost in that jungle for many days, I was not afraid of death,' the old man often told Yuri. 'I knew it wasn't my time. When my time comes, I will die. Man cannot escape his fate.'

To Edison Mwenda the war was something that had happened

and was over, and that was all there would ever be to it. After convalescing from his injuries, he had moved on. What he had learned from the war, as he often told Yuri, was that men fight for each other and if necessary, they will die for each other. And when you are a soldier, you simply do what you have to do. Soldiers follow orders.

And as Yuri Mwenda travelled through the city, its centre now guarded by soldiers, and thought of his grandfather and his history teacher, he wondered who the soldiers were protecting, and from what.

# 7

# Things I Thought You Should Know

*Politicians and diapers should be changed*
*frequently and all for the same reason.*
Jose Maria de Eca de Queiroz

One warm evening at the beginning of April my father dropped a bombshell. He didn't tell us that he'd sired an illegitimate child during his wild teenage years or that he had been diagnosed with a terminal disease. What he told us was worse: that he wanted to run in the primaries on the ruling party ticket during the current elections. He wanted, he said, to be his chosen constituency's new MP for ZANU-PF, the revolutionary party. In 2013, he took part in a primary and narrowly lost to the current MP, a local primary schoolteacher named Onward Gushungo. My father thought about contesting the primary as an independent but friends warned him against it. They told him that the reward for disloyalty to the party is political obscurity. Now he has his eye again on the same constituency in Mashangara, his rural home area, which he tells us 'is there for the taking'.

He believes that 'Now, after the *coup d'etat,* there's a new political dispensation. Our politics will ever be the same again.'

But I've heard him err on the side of optimism so many times before that I cannot believe him. What's undeniable is that by the time of the coup, most people wanted the old president out. Over the years, the old man had become intolerant of dissent, and would mercilessly silence all those who dared to oppose him.

Father says that Onward Gushungo has only visited his constituency a handful of times since he was elected in 2013 and, because of his neglect, the area has remained an underdeveloped and drought-prone backwater. I disagree with him because an MP cannot be expected to fund constituency development issues out of his own pocket, otherwise law-makers would end up as destitute as their constituents. Most of our MPs don't go into parliament to better the lives of others, but only their own. 'All those men can see are dollar signs,' my mother opined. I agree. After all, the only reason most cabinet ministers find themselves featured in the media is in connection with one or another corruption scandal.

But my father is right about Onward Gushungo. The only memorable event that has taken place in the Mashangara constituency since his election was his all-weekend celebration party. I was only eleven at the time, but I remember the occasion well. Many beasts were slaughtered and there was much joy and feasting. The event was strictly by invitation and few villagers were allowed at the venue. This was strange, because Mr Onward Gushungo wouldn't have become an MP if those villagers hadn't voted for him. My father was invited but found a convenient excuse not to go – the funeral of a neighbour he hardly knew. He didn't even go to the funeral, preferring to stay at home and drink whisky with friends. They consoled him by telling him that in the primary he'd been by far the better candidate, and Onward Gushungo had only won because he shared the same clan totem as the country's president. This made my father feel so much better that he had brought out another bottle of fifteen-year-old Glenfiddich from his secret stash.

Father, despite his impressive war credentials, has not done very well in life. My elder sister Nnenna says it's because he's an impulsive man prone to what she calls 'knee-jerk reactions'. Nnenna also has no time for my father's party, ZANU-PF – an organisation she accuses of being dedicated to 'political thuggery and social underdevelopment'. Father has tried his hand at numerous business ventures but everything he touches turns to dust. He likes to call himself an 'indigenous businessman'. This simply means he's a Jack-of-all-trades. Nonetheless, I've always admired my father's resilience. He boasts that it's a tribal trait and calls himself the 'hard MaShona type' and tells us that in life one has to grab what's available with both hands. He's proud of his rural roots, always reminding us how tough it was growing up in the arid, unproductive Tribal Trust Lands, as they were called in colonial days. Now they are called Communal Lands, but they remain as impoverished with fewer trees, less water and more people – mostly women – and the men have fled south for greener pastures.

He's confident that when he's elected he will bring prosperity, happiness, peace and progress to the poverty-stricken rural area of his birth. My mother is sceptical but obviously can't say so to his face. She quietly reminds us that if he cannot bring security to a household of five people, how can he do so in a constituency of over thirty thousand? I nod in agreement but do not say that I have noticed that my father's infrequent forays into the political arena are always opportunistic, a move he makes when poverty knocks on our door. And business-wise last year was a bad year. He went into a cooking-oil venture with a Chinese national which folded after a few months, leaving him knee-deep in debt and his partner nowhere to be found.

Next, my father teamed up with some colleagues and bought an apparently lucrative gold mine. However, the over-worked, under-paid miners smuggled out most of the gold which they sold on the black market. So that venture folded, forcing the bank from which my father had taken a loan to attach a house in Highfield. I was heart-sore because my father had always said that as the last-born, I stood to inherit the house after his death, and small as it was, it was potentially mine.

But my father is not bothered by our mother's concerns about his latest political ambitions – not that we have voiced them loudly. He says this time round he has a master plan to ensure that he wins the primary. His main problem is that his ego has always been bigger than his support base. He alienates people with his provocative speeches, a bad habit he picked up from attending the former First Lady's inflammatory, hate-filled gatherings. Indeed, when the former temporarily ruled the roost, my father was one of her most trusted confidantes, accompanying the 'mother of the nation' to all her 'meet the people' rallies. He says that although he fought in the war he has never enjoyed the fruits of his labours. He says a lot of his colleagues died in that war and it's the duty of the survivors to take the country forward, although it's as clear as day his colleagues in government have only ever taken the country backwards.

He says that people like Onward Gushungo are fly-by-night political opportunists, and after the November coup it's about time he also put his foot in the door. He says that all he has to do is bide his time and wait for the loudmouthed, gaffe-prone Gushungo to trip himself up. 'You never interrupt your enemy when he's making a mistake,' he gloats. Sometimes, when he has had a few tots, he sits us down – Nnenna, my older brother Leonard and myself – and tells us about the hardships of the war, and how we should not take for granted the freedom for which others died. He always concludes these pep-talks with the same words: 'These are things I thought you should know. You have a duty to tell your children about our country's history, and they in turn have a duty to tell it to their children, and so on and so forth.'

The announcement of my father's revived political ambitions is bad news for everybody, especially my mother. She says that if you're a politician you get used by the system, and when you reach your sell-by date, it will spit you out like gum. In her opinion, politics is the only profession you enter when you fail at everything else. But she also knows that considerable expense will be involved, which can only cause us grief. She remembers how the 2013 primaries burnt a sizable hole in father's bank account. Besides, contesting a ZANU-PF primary is not for the faint-hearted – it's simply a brutal war, with all manner of unsavoury characters crawling out of the woodwork.

When my father stood against Onward Gushungo in 2013 there were seven other candidates on the ballot paper – including a convicted serial rapist, a brothel owner and a fraudster released from prison by presidential amnesty. An eighth candidate was disqualified after he was exposed as a fully paid-up member of the Movement for Democratic Change, the opposition party. 'My husband has tried and failed in politics,' my mother tells her friends; she thinks he should now concentrate on trying to make money. As usual, our household expenses are on a tight rein. My older brother Lenny, who is studying for his A-levels, wants to study architecture in Australia, but my father has told him that he will have to make do with one of the local tertiary institutions. 'If the First Lady can get a doctorate at a local university,' he told my mother, 'what's so special about that boy of ours? He won't enjoy living in Australia. I should know; I've been there.'

The most worrying thing for me about my father's decision is that our elections are always violent, because nobody wants to lose. After all, it's an open secret that the 2008 election was lost by Mr Robert Mugabe. Yet he still proclaimed himself the winner and unashamedly participated in a bogus inauguration at State House. It should have been end-game for the old president, but the violence of his tactics revealed his determination to survive at all costs. Many supporters of the opposition were killed or made homeless. Others, fearing for their lives, went into long exile. I remember watching the old man on television, speaking at a rally during that bloody election campaign:

*'A piece of paper can never be allowed to determine our destiny. We will never allow an event like an election to reverse our independence, our sovereignty. Never...'*

Most of our elections are greeted with scepticism because they always go against the grain of public opinion. Still, like my father, Nnenna blames everything on our old enemy, the British. She's completing her final year at university, studying political science, but lives at home because father can't afford to have her stay in residence. He also believes that too much freedom is not a good thing for young women, because too many naive young girls at the universities are impregnated by powerful old men who promise to pass them in their exams. Nnenna, who had really wanted to stay in hall with all her friends, was disappointed and sulked for weeks.

Like our father, Nnenna is against multi-party democracy, arguing that it divides nations and creates weak governments. She is a devoted supporter of deposed despots – Saddam Hussein, Muammar Gaddafi and Nicolae Ceauşescu. My sister is the only person I know who supports Al Qaeda and Boko Haram. She argues that before colonialism, when a chief died, the throne was passed on to the next person in line – the eldest son. If the chief had no sons, the throne would pass on to one of his brothers or male cousins. There was never a question of an outsider or a commoner being elevated to the chieftainship. Still, that said, when Robert Mugabe wanted to anoint his wife as his successor, Nnenna was one of the most vocal opponents of that idea. I shouldn't have been surprised. She has never been one for female chiefs!

One evening my father tells us some good news. After twenty years of trying, he has finally won a government tender to supply water treatment chemicals to the Harare City Council. My father tells us that he is flying to Guangzhou in China, to attend to the pre-shipment formalities. He says he cannot afford to take any chances with such unexpected good fortune. The news is a welcome tonic. We are all so excited that supper is barely eaten. Then, father says that this unexpected windfall will be useful later in the year, when, as the ruling party's parliamentary candidate, he will be able to afford to buy 'campaign material'. This dims our excitement, as we all had plans for how the money might be spent, and not on campaign material.

Father spent ten days in Guangzhou. He phoned several times, usually in the middle of the night because of the time difference. He told us that he avoided going to the hotel restaurant because he saw a photograph of a dog on the menu. He said there was a McDonald's quite close by and he didn't mind surviving on hamburgers. On his return, he tells us that he's ready to embark on his new political journey. He has acquired all the necessary paperwork to get paid a part of his deposit for the tender. We all realise that winning the tender has changed him. There's a spring in his step, confidence in his voice and a mild arrogance in his manner. He has also become intolerant of people he considers socially inferior – street vendors, waiters and petrol attendants. And he's optimistic about his chances in the primaries because his old enemy, Onward Gushungo, was dealt a body blow when the former president, with whom he shares a clan totem, was abruptly removed from power. There were many people like Onward who relied heavily on such patronage, who were left high and dry after the coup.

Gushungo and my father are supposed to belong to the same party, yet they disparage each other at every available opportunity. Neither of them seems to have a clue about the party manifesto – if there is one. Instead of working for the good of their party, they abuse each other. During the 2013 primary, Gushungo denigrated my father as a 'disgruntled political nonentity'. Not to be outdone, my father gave an interview to a state-controlled newspaper and accused his adversary of being a 'gay gangster'. He also said Gushungo was an 'opposition functionary masquerading as a ZANU-PF loyalist'. My father says he lost the 2013 primary to Gushungo because of repeat voting, vote-buying and intimidation. He told our mother that one man he knew told him that he voted five times at five different polling stations, simply by going back to his house and changing his clothes.

'Mukanya, why didn't you report him to the authorities?'

'He was voting for me.'

But now that he will be embarking on political rallies, my father wants to get ready. New suits have to be purchased, as well as platform shoes to make him look taller on makeshift rural podiums.

He suffers from what Nnenna calls the 'short man syndrome'. The election campaign will be gruelling, he tells us, a test of a man's mental and physical strength. He's planning an exploratory 'meet the people' rally, to test the political waters. He says he just wants to make sure he has all his ducks in a row. In life, he tells us, those who triumph are the ones who learn from their mistakes. He says going to the rural constituency is critical because it is important to remember one's roots, just as when drinking water, one has to remember the spring where it came from. But the day before the rally he comes home with a long face.

'Gushungo has been maligning me. He has been spreading the rumour that the only way I can win the primary is by vote-buying.'

'Everybody knows he's the one who buys votes. Don't worry too much. Such talk is the product of lazy tongues.' Mother, as always, is the reliable hydrant that extinguishes all our house fires.

'Onward Gushungo is afraid of losing to you. We all know that.'

The day before the rally, my father arranges with his new election agent for the delivery of several boxes packed with basic commodities to give to the villagers. The man replaced Brezhnev Nyanhete, my father's nephew, who was his election agent in the 2013 primary. A long-standing ruling party supporter, Brezhnev's main task had been supervising the gangs of youths who pulled down all the opposition party posters. But the day before the primary, he had misappropriated some of the commodities meant for the Mashangara villagers and disappeared.

After breakfast, my father downs four double tots of whisky, as if to fortify himself for the gruelling day ahead. On the way to the village, bellicose with alcohol, he tells us that that when he becomes an MP there are certain issues that he's going to tackle head-on in the 'august house', as he likes to call parliament. He says it doesn't make sense that people like Onward Gushungo can be MPs for over ten years, when they are not doing anything worthwhile for their constituencies.

'For example, take my friend Comrade Bhaudhi, the guest speaker. He's been an MP for over twenty years but what has he done for his constituency? The roads are in a terrible state and some of the bridges that collapsed during the war thirty-seven years ago have still not been repaired. One wonders what he does with the constituency development funds. We should have limited terms for all MPs, just as we have limited terms for the president. Five years, then you're out...'

Nnenna and I know by heart most of what my father is telling us, so we can tell our children, and they in turn can tell theirs, and so on and so forth. But after a few tots, he is loquacious and in between hiccups, he again outlines his grand political vision and how it smartly dovetails into the 'new dispensation' of the unelected president. Like Nnenna, he is scornful of western democracy, and complains about 'white monopoly capital and the evil machinations of western imperialism'. He also says 'the masses' shouldn't always be allowed to say what they want, because sometimes the majority can be wrong. An old ZANU hand, he believes in the authority of the vanguard. 'The new president said Zimbabwe is open for business,' he tells us, as he has often done before, 'but that doesn't include insulting our leaders.'

Talking of business, my father is in partnership with the guest speaker, Comrade Everlasting Bhaudhi, who has often been to our house accompanied by his wife Corinne, a plump Irish woman with wild blonde hair. Comrade Bhaudhi is pompous and arrogant – a typical ruling party *chef*. Like my father, he's also partial to single malt whisky. The two of them can sit for hours discussing factional politics over a bottle of Glenfiddich, and whenever they attend party functions together, they hold hands, so that everybody can see how close they are. Of course, out of earshot, my father has many uncomplimentary things to say about his comrade-in-arms, Bhaudhi.

I've been to Bhaudhi's offices on a number of occasions. Men in smart suits and dark sunglasses lurk in the corridors and eye all visitors with suspicion. Comrade Bhaudhi's office has soft burgundy leather settees and an impressive mahogany conference table. His walls are covered with framed certificates: Balance Sheets for Beginners, Leadership Made Simple, Basic Macro-finance for Indigenous Entrepreneurs, and so on. On my first visit, he watched me complacently as I admired the framed photographs of him with the now former First Lady. After the *coup d'etat,* I noticed that these photos had all been replaced by ones of Comrade Bhaudhi posing with members of the military junta that had deposed the First Lady's husband.

I can sense that my mother is anxious to say something. She pretends not to be interested in politics, but Nnenna and I suspect that she secretly supports the opposition. I once eavesdropped on a conversation between my mother and Auntie Gwendolyn Banda, one of her church mates whom Nnenna calls an 'energy vampire'. My mother told her clearly that only an idiot would vote for ZANU-PF in the forthcoming harmonised elections, and Auntie Gwen agreed, although I know that she and her husband Uncle Zachariah can no longer vote because they are classified as 'aliens'.

The truth is that when it comes to politics, my mother is fiercely independent. For instance, she has a deep-rooted mistrust of the Zimbabwe Electoral Commission, the body that oversees the elections. She adjusts her posture and noisily clears her throat.

'Mukanya, you remember that day we watched the army spokesman announcing the coup on TV?'

When my mother is in a confrontational mood she addresses her husband by his totem, a ploy designed to lure him into a sense of false security.

'Yes...'

'You remember he said the president was safe, and they were only targeting the criminals around him?'

'Yes...'

'Well, it's almost five months. How many criminals have they arrested?'

'These things take time, Maude. You can't just go and arrest people when you haven't completed the necessary investigations...'

'Surely, for them to say there are criminals around the president, they must know who the criminals are?'

'Yes, but in a court of law you need dockets and witnesses...'

'But it's been nearly five months, Mukanya...'

Nnenna and I had also watched the televised announcement of the 'military putsch', as my sister likes to call the coup. At the time, she dismissed the proposed mass arrests as a pointless exercise. 'They would need to arrest every MP,' she declared; 'the majority of our politicians are career criminals.' However, the only person they did arrest was the Minister of Finance. We saw him on TV being escorted into a prison van handcuffed and in leg-irons, like a dangerous Wild West bandit. My mother pushes her seat back to give herself more leg-room, as if preparing herself for a final twist of the knife. Long drives always seem to give her time to think that she does not have otherwise.

'And another thing, Mukanya, nothing has really changed since the coup. For example, all the people in the ZEC are hand-picked party supporters. With such an uneven playing field, ZANU-PF will always win. Democracy should be for everybody...'

'There's nothing wrong with the playing field.' My father sounds irritated. 'A soccer team that loses will always say the referee is biased. And, besides, why are these so-called opposition parties always in disagreement with the ZEC?'

'And why is the ruling party always in agreement?'

'Come on Maude, you know that's not true...'

'Okay, if Robert Mugabe was supposed to have two terms, how come he stayed for thirty-seven years?'

'That man kept changing the constitution to prolong his hold on power. It wasn't that clever, because most of us could see what he was doing.'

'So why didn't you do something about it?'

'Yes, maybe it was our fault. But when a person has power, it's difficult to remove him. The new guy knows we are watching his every move. I just hope it doesn't happen again. God will guide the country out of its current hardships.'

My mother snorts.

'Perhaps now we have learnt that to expect God to do everything while we do nothing is not faith but superstition,' she says sharply.

Out of respect, Nnenna and I never participate in our parents' discussions, but I don't think it's fair for my mother to say that apathetic people expect God to do everything for them. Yet sometimes it's not easy to separate faith from superstition. Especially in Africa, where the very people who believe in witchcraft are the ones who attend the Christian churches. Like my mother. Like Aunt Gwen Banda.

The coup was exciting, but apart from the removal of the corrupt traffic police, nothing much has changed. Nnenna is one of the few people I know who benefitted directly from it. In January she wrote a brilliant opinion piece, Pomp & Blasphemy: How Gucci Grace brought down Bob's Empire. The article appeared in a tabloid South African Sunday newspaper and Nnenna was paid so handsomely she invited some of her varsity friends for a braai at the house. Lenny didn't want to come to the rural areas because he had friends coming to our house. So I'm sitting in the back seat of the double-cab Toyota Hilux truck with Nnenna. She's pretending to read a novel which she picked up from a second-hand book stall at the flea market. I know she's pretending to read because every time I glance at her, she's stuck on the same page. It's just her way of isolating herself. When my sister doesn't want to talk, her silence can be like a monastic vow.

We're all wearing the ruling party's gaudy party regalia, except her. She's wearing a white T-shirt with the inscription 'I don't trip: I do random gravity checks'. Nnenna uses inscribed T-shirts to convey her inner sentiments. I remember the day Donald Trump won the American election she spent the day wearing a T-shirt that said 'Elect a Clown, Expect a Circus'. We're about ten kilometres from the rally venue and my father is on the phone, talking to the advance team about the commodities to be given to the villagers. He puts the call on speaker-phone, so we can all hear the conversation. His election agent, Comrade Goriyati Mabhaibhiri, says that everything has gone according to plan, and all the food packs to be distributed after the rally have been safely locked away in a shed.

He says Comrade Bhaudhi has already arrived and is mingling with the villagers, dishing out party regalia. What he doesn't say is that Comrade Bhaudhi is telling everyone that the goodies have come from the party, not my father.

'But chef, there's something else you should know,' says Comrade Goriyati, 'they've put stickers…' But my father impatiently cuts him off in mid-sentence.

'Let's make sure we stick to the programme, Comrade Goriyati. That's what I pay you for. Some big chefs will be coming to that rally.'

Then he turns to my mother, a tremor of excitement in his voice.

'Did you hear that, Maude? The guest of honour has already arrived. I wonder what Gushungo will say when he hears about this rally. I'm sure he'll be quaking in his boots.'

My mother doesn't answer. She knows anyway that after several whiskies, my father will not listen to her. But she also knows that even though the former president is no longer powerful, Onward Gushungo still has friends in high places; friends whose paths my father has crossed. Nnenna, of course, has a theory about what she calls the ruling party's 'fair weather alliances'.

'Political friends are like shadows,' she says. 'They follow you in the sun but leave you in the dark. And you should remember that in politics there're no permanent friends, Jacob, only permanent interests.'

I tend to agree with her: only your true friends will tell you when your face is dirty.

During long journeys, my mother takes off her shoes because her feet tend to swell. She starts doing the stretching exercises she learnt on Air Zimbabwe, to get the blood circulating again. We can now see the rally venue in the distance – three huge white tents spread across the base of a small hill in the midday haze, like the sails of tall ships. My mother finishes her exercises and puts her shoes back on. After we arrive, our parents sit in the VIP tent whilst Nnenna and I remain in the truck. Amidst subdued ululations, my father steps onto the stage and delivers his speech. He tells the crowd that freedom of speech is something that needs to be carefully managed, to stop people going around saying what they want or insulting their leaders. He concludes by saying that capitalism is an evil system designed to enrich a few people at the expense of the majority. Nnenna turns to me, yawns, and loudly reads out a passage from her book:

'Capitalism is essentially psychopathic. It lives for the moment, and all larger questions of morality are delegated to patriotism, religion or psychoanalysis.'

At the end of the rally, Comrade Bhaudhi gives a short vote of thanks, as if he's in a hurry to leave. My mother and the other dignitaries applaud politely. As soon as he sits down, there's a frenzied scramble for the hand-outs which is really the only reason why villagers attend the rallies. The guests in the VIP tent watch in astonishment. Dozens of loaves of bread, crushed in the melée, are immediately rendered inedible. Torn packets of flour dust people's heads and faces white as they jostle to grab whatever's on offer. One elderly man has fainted, and two women are trying to revive him. Minutes later, our parents join us in the truck and we prepare to depart. Then Comrade Mabhaibhiri hurries over to the driver's side and my father lowers his window.

'Chef Makanda, what I was trying to tell you on the phone is that Comrade Bhaudhi told the crowd that the party donated all the foodstuffs.'

'But that's not true,' my father says bitterly. 'I bought everything here with my own money.'

'We know that, chef. But there's also another problem...'

'What problem?' Father's speech is slurred. He must have consumed more Glenfiddich in the VIP tent.

'It's about your CV...'

'My CV?'

'I'm told it wasn't accepted. They're saying you're not eligible to run in the primaries next weekend.'

'Who's saying that?'

'The people from the National Commissariat.'

'There's nothing wrong with my CV. Everybody knows who I

am. Everybody knows I fought in the war.'

'We all know that, chef...'

'So, what exactly is the problem?'

'When you were in China, the provincial co-ordinating committee drew up a list of people who were known to be part of the former First Lady's faction, and your name is on it.'

'My name is on it?'

'Yes, chef...'

'Why?'

'They claim you were a key member of the G40 cabal...'

'Me? A member of the G40? What a ridiculous suggestion!'

'I know. The primary election is next weekend, but your name is not on the ballot paper, chef.'

'That's preposterous...'

'When you were in China, a video clip showing you at one of the former First Lady's rallies went viral on social media.'

I remember the video clip from Facebook. My mother, who is active on numerous WhatsApp groups, was sent that clip so many times she eventually switched off her cellphone. My father is not into social media, always telling us that WhatsApp and Twitter are the main tools used by his party's enemies to spread fake news. So in our household, we never share anything on social media with him because most of it is uncomplimentary about ZANU-PF.

'So what? ZANU-PF is full of hypocrites. Who didn't attend that stupid woman's rallies? Comrade Bhaudhi went to those rallies, so did most of the cabinet ministers. The new president, when he was the VP, went to those rallies and sat on the high table smiling while that crazy woman insulted him. In fact, he only stopped attending when he was fired and had to go into exile.'

'We all know that, chef...'

'How can I not be on the ballot? It's Onward Gushungo up to his mud-slinging tricks again, isn't it? This primary is just a shambolic plebiscite, and I can assure you it will be the precursor to the party's Waterloo. I'll put a stop to these clandestine and nonsensical imbroglios...'

When my father is angry, he uses big words, not always correctly. The angrier he is, the bigger the words.

'They only told us this morning that your CV had been rejected, chef...'

'Where's Comrade Bhaudhi?

'He's already left, sir. He said he had to pass by Mashangara business centre.'

'What's there?'

'Comrade Gushungo is having a rally there. Chef Bhaudhi has to give the vote of thanks.'

'Is Bhaudhi aware of this CV nonsense?'

'I'm told he's the one who instructed that your name be withdrawn from the ballot.'

'Bhaudhi?'

'Yes, chef...'

'When did he do this?'

'I understand it was a few day ago, when the district leadership held a meeting. I was not invited to that meeting, chef.'

'They can't do this to me. I'll expose Bhaudhi and Gushungo. Did you know those two men are not even citizens of this country? First thing tomorrow morning, I'll go and see the party's national political commissar. That man is my friend – he and I were in the bush together during the war. I can assure you that I'll be on that ballot paper come next weekend. These people are playing with fire, and I'll put an end to this nonsense.'

We leave soon afterwards. Mother, after removing her shoes shuts her eyes. Nnenna is busy texting. Father, apart from the occasional hiccup, is unusually quiet. The bad news seems to have jolted him into instant sobriety. I wonder what is going through his mind, now that his political dream seems to have been crushed again and he has been betrayed by men he thought were his friends. He often tells us that there are things that we should know, but it appears as if there are also intrigues in his own political party that he should have known. After all, he's well versed in their cloak-and-dagger politics: or, to quote my cynical sister: 'the entrenched interests of aged politicians and the arrogant posturing of the war vets who believe their participation in the struggle entitles them to exclusive ownership of the country from one generation to the next'.

On the way back, we pass excited villagers, carrying packets of rice or maize meal on their heads. Most are wearing T-shirts carrying a portrait of Onward Gushungo and the caption 'Onward ever, backward never'. They seem to be going to the MP's evening rally at Mashangara business centre. In the bright beam of the truck's headlights they're hunched and white-faced, like escapees from a leper colony. It seems my father has lost his latest fight with his perennial nemesis. But with the primaries still a week away, I'm confident he will find a way out of his current predicament. He's a resourceful man, Comrade Howard Ludovic Makanda – a hard MaShona type – and always rises to the occasion. But then again, maybe his destiny is not to become a ZANU-PF member of parliament. As Nnenna says, in politics, moral degradation is unavoidable – and you can't win a bet against fate.

# 8

# A New Dispensation

*He who allows oppression shares the crime*
Desiderius Erasmus

*Wednesday, 1ˢᵗ August 2018*

That morning was the fifth time in two years that the youths had marched from the opposition head office to the Rainbow Towers Hotel, where the Zimbabwe Electoral Commission was due to announce the election results. Led by Edmore Chidzonga, an unemployed graduate who scraped a living by selling imported second-hand clothes, the two dozen or so young men trooped towards the hotel, located just beyond the city centre.

They were driven by anger and suspicion caused by the repeated postponement of the presidential election results. They knew that this was certainly not the first time the ruling party had stolen the election from the opposition. But no election result had ever been annulled or reversed, no matter how much rigging was exposed in court. The judges, after all, benefited from the system.

'They want to steal our votes again,' Edmore told his mates as they walked to the hotel, 'as they have done at every election. But this time we must stand up and tell the ZEC that enough is enough.'

Although the harmonised elections held two days previously had been peaceful, a restive nation now awaited the presidential results. During a press conference the commission's chairwoman, a high court judge with an imperious manner and flamboyant dress sense, skilfully dodged the journalists' probing questions and repeatedly reminded them that there had been twenty-three presidential candidates. Most, it was believed, had been paid to stand by the ruling party to create just these diversions.

However, the ZEC chairwoman's condescending manner failed to allay the growing suspicions that something sinister was afoot. The commission's tactics of announcing results in selective batches had not alleviated any fears. Social media users had already identified glaring anomalies. A constituency in the south, with more sugar-cane plants than people, had recorded the highest number of votes for the ruling party. Opposition polling agents pointed to constituencies with several hundred more ballot papers than registered voters. There were rumours that agents who'd photographed results at the polling stations had had to run for their lives when armed militia tried to seize their phones threatening death at their hands. The election campaign, characterised as it was by empty sloganeering and pie-in-the-sky promises by both main parties, had been largely peaceful. But everyone knew that were the opposition to win, the ruling party would resort to violence. They had claimed the country in a civil war against their colonial masters, and now regarded it as their own.

*Monday, 1ˢᵗ August 2016*

The last occasion Edmore and his colleagues had marched to the Rainbow Towers had been exactly two years earlier when they had demonstrated against 'corruption in high places'. Choosing the hotel where the second vice-president chose to stay at the taxpayers' expense had seemed an appropriate venue. As usual, Edmore Chidzonga had been at the front of the march, holding aloft a banner that read 'Government stop stealing from the poor'. At twenty-six, Edmore had become a very vocal presence in Youths

Against Poverty. Repeatedly arrested, and often beaten or thrown into the filthy police cells, Edmore's belief in his constitutional right to freedom of expression remained undeterred. And on this occasion, he was buoyed up by the hope that the opposition had won. If there was change, his future would be secure. He would get a job, and thereafter lay a future. He had even promised his wife that when this happened, he would cease to protest. She worried about his wellbeing, often having to nurse his baton-battered body as he could not afford to go to a hospital. She was frightened and tired of the threatening phone calls and the mysterious cars that drove slowly drive past their one-roomed home. And she did not want her husband to die fighting for freedom. It was a concept that meant little to her, as nothing in her short life had ever been free.

## Wednesday, 1ˢᵗ August 2018

At about ten in the morning, the small group of YAP protesters made it to the front entrance of the Rainbow Towers hotel, only to find the gates locked and a truck full of riot police parked in front of the hotel. They held up placards demanding that the ZEC should release the presidential election results and shouted the claims of their leaders – that what was emerging from the vote count was a co-ordinated and systematic pattern of premeditated electoral fraud. An hour later, the crowd massed in front of the hotel had grown, and included some rowdy criminal elements that began throwing an assortment of crude missiles at the police truck. Sensing an opportunity to vent their frustrations, hordes of belligerent street vendors soon appeared from all corners of the central business district.

The riot police, their patience exhausted by the relentless taunting, dismounted and gave chase to the demonstrators. Smoke from teargas canisters spiralled skywards, turning the early spring air acrid. A water cannon malfunctioned, releasing gallons onto the streets. Within minutes several truckloads of soldiers in full combat gear appeared, firing live ammunition. Mayhem ensued. Bodies fell. The crowd ran this way and that. Police and army were on every corner. The fleeing demonstrators were driven between them, like impalas being cornered by a pack of wild dogs. A lone army helicopter hovered in the clear blue sky above the battle zone, whilst on the ground an armoured car streaked down Rotten Row to an unknown destination.

A portly woman, felled in a fusillade of bullets, lay in a twitching heap on the pavement. A group of soldiers cornered an elderly man and his wife and pummelled them with the butts of their rifles. As the soldiers advanced towards the fleeing horde, it was clear who was in charge. The message being delivered was unequivocal: the country belonged to those who claimed to have liberated it, not to those for whom it had been liberated. The veneer of legitimacy with which the military government had tried to win over the support of the international community was stripped bare in twenty minutes of trigger-happy madness.

Later that evening, after the disturbances had abated, Edmore and eight of his colleagues were rounded up by the police at the MDC's head office on Nelson Mandela Avenue, where they had sought refuge. They were taken to the Rotten Row magistrates' court and charged with the usual public order offences. Edmore, who had a little money from the sale of some second-hand clothes, paid his fine and those of two of his colleagues, who had no money. After they were released, Edmore called his wife Marita and told her he was on his way home.

Still nursing his bruised body, he slowly made his way to the Copacabana commuter rank. He had a gash above his right eye, a badly bruised thigh and he could taste blood in his mouth. He had lost both shoes and was walking barefoot. The police had regrouped and a sombre calm had been restored in the city centre. Usually, the commuter rank would have been buzzing with rush-hour activity. But today, the whole area was deserted, save for a few vendors sheltering fearfully in the dark alcoves of shuttered doorways. The ubiquitous commuter kombis and the illegal short-hop taxis known as *mshikashika* had all disappeared. Even the street kids, who daily begged at traffic intersections, had vanished. Edmore wondered how he would get home, but he was grateful to be alive.

He had learnt from social media that six civilians had been killed in the disturbances, with dozens more injured. As a blood-red moon emerged on the distant horizon, Edmore Chidzonga realised that whatever the outcome of the election, his life was not going to change. He remembered how his late grandfather often told him that *tsuro haipone rutsva kaviri*; a hare can only escape a bush fire once. He had spent six years protesting. Six years claiming his right to speak out, his right to work; six years protesting the corrupt elite who lives in mansions on five-acre plots, while 'the masses' were crowded into shacks and hovels in dirty potholed streets. For the first time, he felt he had no future.

# Epilogue: Fallen Kingdom

*Sunday, 19ᵗʰ November 2017*

It is well past midnight, five days after the coup. Anselmo Ganyanga is packing his few belongings whilst absentmindedly watching the local TV channel. It is reported that later that day, parliament will begin impeachment proceedings against the president, something that would have been unthinkable only a week earlier. Now floundering in a miasma of his own making, the president has no option but to resign. For a man often hailed as a deity by his acolytes, impeachment offers an ignominious exit. It's a taste of his own medicine, having once done to the vice-president just what is now being done to him: an unceremonious end to an inglorious reign by a man who had sworn he would die in office. And yet Anselmo has mixed feelings about this latest development. An ardent and life-long admirer of the president, he feels like a man who is about to lose a much treasured family heirloom.

*Wednesday, 15ᵗʰ November 2017*

Anselmo had arrived at the Hollywood Lodge shortly before half-past five on that cold wet morning. The double-storey building stood in the seediest part of the Avenues. The passage of time had taken its toll, but the miscellany of worn structures retained a stubborn, decrepit elegance. The reception area was a dark, sparsely furnished space, the curtains were discoloured and every metallic object in the room had lost its lustre. The rooms could be booked on an hourly, daily or weekly rate. Discretion was the Hollywood Lodge's core tenet. Once guests had paid their money, it was each sinner to their own fault.

The morning after the coup the streets of the capital were eerily quiet, with fewer people than normal going about their daily routines. It was as if the nation was waking up from a long nightmare and struggling to disentangle its disparate emotions. The military, for so long restless and politically abused, seemed to have wrestled power from a kingdom in crisis. Newspaper vendors stood at familiar roadside intersections, staring despairingly at the piles of unsold newspapers. Nobody was interested in yesterday's news, now it had been overtaken by the night's unexpected events. People huddled in small groups underneath shop-front awnings, speaking in hushed tones. Astonishingly, there was a total absence of traffic police. These officers, corrupt to the core, had become uniformed highway predators. Always lascivious for their daily pound of flesh, they spared no one. Inevitably, among the toadying elite whose contempt for the poor knew no bounds, there were concerns that the disappearance of the police might lead to rioting and looting. They knew that populist anger, like water, always follows the path of least resistance.

Anselmo was a man on the run but, at that moment, he was not sure what he was running away from. He needed time to sit, reflect, and come up with a plan about his now uncertain future. The previous night he had been unable to sleep, making frequent visits to the bathroom. Normally it was his wife Monica, a chronic insomniac, who lay awake all night. A beautiful but tormented woman, she had silently endured his philandering ways throughout their turbulent thirty-year union. Anselmo eventually went downstairs and flicked through the satellite television channels. His heart stopped when he saw two grim-faced men behind the desk normally occupied by the evening newsreader on the local channel. One was dressed in army fatigues, the other in the light blue shirt of the country's air force. He could not believe what he was hearing:

'*The situation in our country has moved to another level...*'

A coup! Anselmo was aghast and disbelieving. His heart was racing, and his plans for the day went up in smoke. As a government speech-writer, he was supposed to be at his office early to prepare a speech for his new boss, a cabinet minister, who was officiating at the ground-breaking ceremony of a rural clinic later that day. He was also required to prepare a speech for the First Lady's next rally ear-marked for the following weekend, a task that had filled him with considerable trepidation. Although he had honed his speech-writing art into a consummate copy-and-paste exercise, he still needed to leaf through his archives and decide which old speeches to recycle for both his boss and the First Lady. The former wasn't particularly bright and, like most of his ministerial counterparts, owed his cabinet post to patronage rather than competence. Usually, he just read what was put in front of him.

The president's wife also never read any of her prepared speeches, preferring instead to deliver the vitriolic and rambling spur-of-the-moment monologues that had become her trademark. After another quick glance at the two stony-faced officers, Anselmo switched off the television and tiptoed back to the bedroom to collect his cellphone and wallet, the two personal items around which his whole life revolved. Monica reacted to the slightest disturbances and he was anxious not to disturb her. But this time she was already awake, holding the television remote in her hand the way one would a loaded but unpredictable gun. In his brief absence, she had switched on the bedroom TV and watched the same live broadcast that he had been listening to downstairs. He looked at her and shook his head.

'The military has taken over.'

She nodded.

'I need to leave right away. With my connections to the First Family, the soldiers will definitely come looking for me. It's not safe for me to stay here.'

'Whatever you say, *Mhofu*. You know best.'

His frequent but unexplained absences had always been a feature of their troubled marriage, but this time she seemed to understand the need for his hasty departure. However, after leaving his house, Anselmo had been in a state of confusion. He didn't know what to do, or where to go. But there is no force stronger than that of self-preservation. Driven by instinct, he had initially gone to Mbare, the township where he grew up. These occasional trips to the township were journeys in search of spiritual redemption, the penitential pilgrimages of a prodigal son returning to his roots. He spent some time in a bar, which was still open at that late hour. People were talking about football and about the shocking prices of basic commodities, but nobody was talking about the coup.

He left the bar shortly after dawn. Although he had driven to the township, he decided to leave his car at a city centre hotel's car park. When he left his house, aware that government-issued vehicles could be easily identified from their registration plates, he had opted not to use his official Mercedes. Instead, he had taken his wife's vehicle, a second-hand Japanese import. He was confident the car would be inconspicuous in the jungle of Ipsums, Spacios, Fun Cargos and Nadias that clogged the hotel's guarded car park. To give himself time to realign his scrambled thoughts, he took a winding route to the lodge, located on the southern edge of the Avenues.

As he walked down Fourth Street towards Robert Mugabe Road, he took stock of how much had changed. The social disparities could not be more glaring, the economic polarisations more frightening. Perhaps this was the true legacy of the man the army had just deposed. It was no longer the genteel, sleepy metropolis of his younger years, with its quaint British cars snaking up and down the dipping avenues named after the country's colonists – Rhodes, Jameson, Stanley, Baker and Forbes. All around him, the city's new tribes lined the pavements, their wares spread out on the ground. Over the years, vendors had steadily arrived from all four corners of the country, brazenly staking a permanent foothold in the very heart of the capital – as if daring those they held responsible for their tragic uprooting and unemployment to an inevitable but decisive confrontation. Everything around Anselmo looked old and wasted. Even the jacaranda trees had aged, their branches gnarled beyond recognition, their leaves calloused with the pollution of decades and their trunks inscribed with the crude messages of passing schoolboys and public declarations of spurned lovers. Like those displaced people, Anselmo had also known the fear of alienation. Moreover, when he allowed himself to admit it, he too had been running away from shameful secrets all his life.

As he wandered aimlessly around the indistinct peripheries of the city, it was clear to Anselmo that the military's intended targets were the First Lady and her known acolytes. He kept anxiously checking his phone for the latest up-dates. The news filtering through his numerous WhatsApp groups was not good. The news blackout imposed by the military had inadvertently allowed social media platforms to go into overdrive. Speculative scenarios abounded, ranging from the palpably credible to the downright outlandish. Eventually, he arrived at the lodge, as if his feet knew better than his head, and he checked himself in determined to sit out the next few days until the situation became clearer.

The following morning he remained cocooned in his stuffy room, going through the text messages that were coming thick and fast on his cellphone. The more disturbing information came from his work colleagues. It seems as if the military has been systematically rounding up the First Lady's known sympathisers. Her once powerful faction was now in disarray, incredible as that might seem.

Things were falling apart very rapidly for the old president and his impetuous young wife, now apparently both under house arrest. In the preceding months those closest to the wife had gently warned her to tone down her acidic rhetoric, advising her that in the country's volatile and unpredictable politics, it was more important to make friends than enemies. A vain, pompous and arrogant woman, she had begun acting as if she was the one with executive powers. Well-known for her profligate ways, she spent most of her time living the good life in foreign lands. When back home, she convened regular gatherings where mobs cheered her increasingly absurd pronouncements. It now seemed her fall was inevitable. Sands shift. Kingdoms rise and kingdoms fall.

At lunchtime, Anselmo ordered room service, a toasted chicken-mayo sandwich and fruit juice. Moments later, he tossed the sandwich into the small plastic bin in a corner of the room in a gesture that seemed to reflect the futility of the moment. Feeling nauseous, he watched a foreign news channel on the television. At last, it seemed as if the slow motion coup was gathering pace. All the major foreign news channels seemed to have something substantive to say about the military takeover. As usual, a plethora of doom-and-gloom pundits had been roped in to provide expert analysis on the unfolding events. But the fate of the deposed president and his immediate family remained uncertain. Some said he had skipped the country, others thought he was still holed up in his blue-roofed mansion. An unproven rumour on social media claimed the old president had been taken ill, his house arrest having triggered a cardiac arrest.

Later that afternoon, Anselmo took a cold shower and sat by the window. A group of the lodge's female patrons seated in the courtyard were discussing the unfolding political drama in loud, inebriated voices. Anxious for the latest news, he dressed quickly and went to sit at a table adjacent to the girls. Munching potato crisps and sipping a Coke, he eavesdropped on their conversation. But moments later, the girls, all of them now quite tipsy, picked up their glasses and walked bee-line into the over-crowded bar. Dejected that his eavesdropping had yielded no new information, he slowly walked back to his room. Restless and distracted, he took a calculated risk and called his wife Monica on his house's landline. He caught her just before she went to bed. He could visualise her going through her vast collection of pirated DVD's, selecting the ones to help her fight her insomnia.

'Have the soldiers come looking for me?'

'No, *Mhofu*.'

'Are you sure?'

'Of course I'm sure, *Mhofu*. I live here.'

Sensing her combative mood, he quickly concluded the conversation. During their frequent verbal wars, she let him know that she was aware of his infidelities, but that her silence did not mean he was beyond reproach and nor did it signify her acquiescence. That evening he sat alone in a secluded corner of the courtyard, having his supper. Across the courtyard was a popular bar known by its regulars as the Aljazeera, because of its reputation for the malicious gossip of its patrons and the daily dissemination of fake news by the barmen. He sent his wife a text message, asking her whether soldiers had been to the house looking for him. She responded by telling him that the only visitor to the house that day was a debt collector from the city council. Most of the conversations around him seemed to be about the coup, some of the patrons not being impressed by the new order. For them, the fact that the ruling party would remain in power was like a snake shedding its old skin – the markings on the new skin would be the same.

Anselmo sensed that the country hung precipitately on a knife-edge. It seemed as if, after years of being abused by one selfish man who ruled his impoverished nation with a feudal fist, the restive but cowed nation had become like patients in the final stages of a corrosive illness. He had always gone to the lodge for *sadza* and boiled cow heels with other government officials. Now, on his own, he suddenly felt like an unwanted intruder, an animal that has strayed too far outside its familiar turf. He stared at the empty bed, at the bare walls, at the stained and threadbare bedspread with its elaborate Queen of Hearts motifs. Hoping for fresh news, he kept track of developments through his WhatsApp groups. But all normal programme schedules had been suspended, and the radio stations were playing old revolutionary songs from the country's liberation struggle. He was worried about Monica, but when he left he had told her not to contact him, as there was no way of knowing who could be listening in on the calls. Over the years, his matrimonial difficulties had degenerated into a war of sullen silences.

*Saturday, 18<sup>th</sup> November 2017*

Anselmo is sitting next to the window in his room, eavesdropping on conversations in the courtyard. The Aljazeera bar girls are occupying their usual table. They never seem to sleep. He has witnessed many catfights amongst them, but the protagonists always tearfully made up, as if bound by the unshakeable code of their mafia sisterhood. They seemed to agree that it was the First Lady's impetuosity which has cost her husband his job. Anselmo agrees, having known that despite her grandiose pretensions, the First Lady was always going to be a political lightweight. Her illusions far outweighed her capabilities. No matter how many press-ups a lizard does, it can never look like a crocodile. He has been awake for most of the night, following developments on the foreign news channels. He has spent another troubled night wondering how a president who had once promised so much had found himself in this invidious position; how unfettered power had made him the face of the tyranny he once fought. In the twilight of his rule, the president's empire had collapsed like a sand castle.

Anselmo's soul-searching had continued until dawn, when he had briefly succumbed to uneasy slumber. He had concluded that the president only had himself to blame, and that his wife's injudicious entry into politics had only been the latest manifestation of the country's gradual drift into the international brotherhood of failed states. But the old president was clearly on the ropes. A cunning populist, he had presided over the almost total destruction of his country's once solid infrastructure by allowing institutionalised corruption and nepotism. The factories had been reduced to empty shells and the roads, long neglected, had become virtually impassable. The public health system had deteriorated to the extent that typhoid, a medieval disease, would occasionally rear its ugly head and kill scores of people in the impoverished and over-crowded townships.

One of the daily papers reported that those now in power had sanctioned a march to be held that very day. Although the event had been called by the country's so-called war vets, many civic groups participated in the march whose purpose was to show solidarity with the military for rescuing the country from the brink of an abyss. Later that day, in typical fashion, the war vets' leader, a verbose and pompous man, would claim exclusive credit for spearheading the ouster of a despot his organisation had always venerated as a deity. Characteristically dismissive of the coup, the beleaguered president was setting impossible conditions for his inevitable departure. The people were aware that despite pursuing disastrous, ill-advised economic policies and possessing a disdainful disregard for human rights, the ousted dictator was still regarded by some of the country's rural citizens as an iconic figure. But even the Devil has his worshippers, his die-hard disciples, his rabid jihadists.

It seemed that even the ousted president's former praise-singers had deserted him, quickly changing their factional colours to match their new surroundings. However, Anselmo understood that in politics betrayal is inevitable, and the only thing that counts is survival. The street celebrations that day attested to the fact the overall message had been delivered loud and clear. People wanted the president and his wife gone. This new revolution was being televised live, for the whole world to see. And the celebrations, a piece of history in the making, were taking place in living rooms, in bars, on buses and on the streets.

*Sunday, 19th November 2017*

Anselmo woke up late that morning. Ordinarily he would have been preparing to go to church with his wife and the youngest of his three daughters. He wasn't a devout Christian, and only went to appease his wife and present a pious face to the world. He was not a man used to the company of strangers and his self-imposed isolation was beginning to take its toll. Going for lunch in the courtyard, he found a free table and ordered a steak and chips. Unlike the chicken, the lodge's steaks were usually fresh and palatable. His major concern was that he was quickly running out of cash and would soon be forced to use his debit card, though he had no idea how much remained in the account.

At sunset he went into the Aljazeera and sat alone in a secluded corner. He ordered a beer, his first alcoholic drink in nearly five days. After another day in lonely reflection, he had finally decided there was nothing to link him directly to the First Lady, other than the few innocuous speeches, which she had not used. After a televised soccer game, there was an unexpected announcement that the president was going to give a live address from the State House. The bar's patrons immediately jostled for the best vantage points. Even the girls vacated their favourite table and came in to watch the broadcast.

This was the moment the whole country had been waiting for – the old president finally announcing his resignation after nearly four decades of iron-fisted rule. The president fumbled with the papers on the desk in front of him, constantly adjusting his spectacles and fidgeting in his seat. Under the glare of the camera lights he cut a pathetic figure. The crowd waited with bated breath. The atmosphere, electric with tension and anticipation, was underpinned by a palpable aura of *shadenfreude.* Vain and aloof, the president pretended the situation in the country was normal, that at the ripe old age of ninety-three he would somehow suddenly find the elusive panacea to fix all the economic and social ills that had vexed the country over the last two decades.

And yet, for a man given to long and disjointed addresses, the speech was uncharacteristically short. Apart from some mollifying sentiments, it lacked substance. It was all pomp and bluster, a manifesto of misrule from an unapologetic, conceited man. After he finished, there was a mixture of anger, confusion and disbelief in the bar. The surreal address had not been the much anticipated valedictory speech. Instead, it had been a red herring: a bizarre epilogue to a remarkable week. One of the bar girls seemed close to tears. She turned to Anselmo.

'What was that last thing he said?'

'*Asante Sana.*'

'What does that mean?'

'It's Swahili for thank you very much.'

'Thanking us for what?'

'I don't know. Maybe for listening to him...'

'So, the old nigger didn't resign?'

'Not in so many words.'

'Oh shit...'

And yet, those who still believed in the embattled president were hopeful of a last minute comeback, like a dubious penalty kick awarded to the losing team in the dying minutes of a difficult match. Anselmo realised how age had dimmed the old man's intellect, how arrogance had made him stubborn and how blind love had eroded his powers of judgment. It seemed the end, like the final act of a Shakespearean tragedy, had duly arrived. Anselmo weighed his ever-dwindling options. He couldn't remain in hiding forever, and he had nowhere to go. He had more to lose leaving the country than staying on and facing the consequences. He knew his life had reached a critical junction, and the decision he was about to make would determine his fate. He soon made up his mind. He would return to his home and his wife. He dialled her number. She answered on the second ring. He instantly knew she has been awake, probably watching the badly dubbed movies on the foreign channels, an addiction she could not shake off.

'Did the soldiers come looking for me?'

'No, *Mhofu*.'

'Are you sure?'

'Of course I'm sure, *Mhofu.*'

'I'm coming home. I'm tired of hiding away.'

'It's up to you, *Mhofu*. You know best.'

He could almost hear her shrugging, as if she understood his latest absence as another episode in their rather boring matrimonial melodrama. His adulterous adventures had long since stopped surprising her and their thirty-year old marriage had become a cycle of fights and reconciliations. Nevertheless, he felt both relief and disappointment that nobody had been looking for him. Down in the courtyard, the bar girls were in a celebratory mood. Slowly and methodically, he packed his few belongings. A few minutes later, he made his way to the front reception. The girls observed him from the shadows, sharp-eyed like raptors. Outside, the early morning air was sharp and crisp. He knew his life, like that of his fellow citizens,would never be the same again. Most of all, he knew the lives of those whose greed brought a once prosperous country to its knees would never be the same again. Because every power is subject to another power and, power, like dew, evaporates.

Printed in the United States
By Bookmasters